The Essential Bible

A Summary of the Major Stories

Third Edition

Bradley C. Jenson
Jill D. Jenson

Azariah Press
Duluth, Minnesota

AZARIAH PRESS
4243 Charles Road
Duluth, MN 55803
Telephone: 218-724-3822
azariah@charter.net

Bradley C. Jenson and Jill D. Jenson

The essential bible, 3rd edition
ISBN 978-1-4507-6571-8

Parlay Enterprises originally published this book (1998).

To Our Parents

Contents

The Old Testament

The New Testament

Preface

Why write a book called *The Essential Bible* when so many versions of the Bible are already available? Because even with all those other versions on the bookstore shelves, something was missing. Nowhere could we find a book that accurately summarizes the most important stories in the Bible in a style that is easy to read and understand and that was *not* written exclusively for children. We wrote *The Essential Bible* to fill that need.

This need first became evident to Brad as a student at Luther Seminary in St. Paul, Minnesota, in 1980. Brad's advisor, Dr. Roy A. Harrisville, Jr., knew that even his eager group of seminary advisees needed a good review of basic Bible content. Dr. Harrisville used copies of a well-worn text, long since out of print, titled *Volrath Vogt's Bible History for Christian Schools*, translated from Norwegian in 1878. Although its language and scholarship were dated, it covered the major stories of the Bible quite well. When Brad became a pastor, he searched for a contemporary teaching resource which offered a similarly excellent summary, but found none. After years of searching, he began to write one himself. Over the next two years and with Jill's help, that work became *The Essential Bible*.

What we discovered during those two years was that it is not only pastors who seek such a resource. *The Essential Bible* was written for a wider audience. First, it was written for anyone who is simply seeking to understand the Bible for the first time. Second, it was written for anyone who strives to help others gain a clearer, deeper understanding of the Bible, including pastors, Bible study leaders, and Sunday School, Confirmation, and seminary instructors. Third, it was written for students, teachers, and anyone else who enjoys the great literature of today and yesterday. Sadly, much of the richness of that literature is lost on readers who fail to recognize the many Biblical allusions and references that so many of our best-known authors use so brilliantly.

No matter what audience you are part of, you should know how *The Essential Bible* was put together. It is organized to reflect the order in which the major stories appear in the Bible itself. This was relatively easy to accomplish with respect to the Old Testament, but the New Testament posed a challenge, both in content and order, because there are four versions of the Gospel of Jesus Christ. Three of them—Matthew, Mark, and Luke—are called the "Synoptic Gospels." While they are very similar, the fourth Gospel, that according to John, tells the story of Jesus in a unique way.

Since Mark was the first gospel to be written, and Matthew and Luke depended heavily on Mark in their telling of the Gospel, Mark was given priority as "first among equals." Therefore, with only a few exceptions, where one of the major gospel stories is told by Mark as well as one or more other gospel writers, we've chosen to give you Mark's version.

Likewise, we chose to reflect the priority of Mark in the organization of the gospel stories. However, a number of major stories do not appear in Mark's gospel. In those instances, with one exception, we chose to follow the order given in the *Synopsis of the Four Gospels*, edited by Kurt Aland (3rd corrected edition, 1979).

Bible references to the original books accompany each major story so that the reader can easily connect the story to the Bible itself. Whenever Bible verses are quoted in their entirety, such as with the Ten Commandments and the Psalms in the Old Testament section and the Sermon on the Mount and the Letters in the New Testament section, they are quoted from the New Revised Standard Version Bible (1989).

The two versions of the Lord's Prayer and the Apostles' and Nicene creeds found in the Appendix are from the *Lutheran Book of Worship* (1978). Although the creeds are not found in the Bible, they are helpful as brief statements of the Christian faith that are based on the Bible.

Finally, we thank Dr. Roy A. Harrisville, Jr., for his invaluable comments, gentle guidance, and constant encouragement as well as Drs. Frank Parker and Kathryn Riley of Parlay Enterprises, the original publishers of this book, without whom it would not have become a reality.

Bradley C. and Jill D. Jenson

March, 2011

THE OLD TESTAMENT

The Beginning

Six Days of Creation and the Sabbath
(Genesis 1–2:4a)

In the beginning, God created the universe. The earth was covered with water and darkness, and God's spirit swept over the water. On the first day of creation, God said, "Let there be light," and light appeared. On the second day, God made a vast expanse, which he called sky. On the third day, God gathered all the waters together into one place, so dry land appeared. He also created plants and fruit trees. On the fourth day, God made the sun to shine during the day and the moon and stars to shine at night. On the fifth day, God created animals that live in the water and others that live on land. He also made birds to fly over the land. On the sixth day, humankind (who would rule over the fish, birds, and other animals) was created in God's likeness. Then God looked at everything he had made and saw that it was all very good. God blessed the seventh day and made it holy because on that day he rested from all the work that had gone into creation.

The Garden of Eden
(Genesis 2:4b–25)

God formed a man from dust, and God breathed into the man's nostrils so that the man was alive. He put the man in Eden, which was a place in the east where God planted a beautiful garden. [The man has been called Adam, and the garden has been referred to as Paradise.] The Lord God made every tree that grew in the garden bear good fruit. A tree called the tree of life grew in the middle of the garden, as did one called the tree of the knowledge of good and evil.

God put the man in the garden of Eden to till it and keep it, but warned Adam, "You are free to eat from every tree in the garden except from the tree of the knowledge of good and evil. If you eat from that tree, you will die."

God saw that it wasn't good for Adam to be alone, so he decided to provide him with a helper to be his partner. God brought all the living creatures to Adam to see what Adam would call them. Adam gave the animals names, but he found no helper to be his partner. So God made Adam fall into a deep sleep. While he slept, God took one of Adam's ribs and made a woman from it. When God brought her to Adam, Adam said, "At last, this one is just like me. I will call her woman, for she was taken out of man." This is why a man leaves his parents to be with his wife, so together they become one flesh. And Adam and his wife were naked, but they were not ashamed.

The First Sin and Its Punishment
(Genesis 3)

Among the animals that God had made was a snake, and this snake was among the most crafty that the Lord created. The snake asked the woman, "Did God tell you not to eat from the trees in the garden?" The woman answered, "We are allowed to eat the fruit in the garden; but God told us we can't eat the fruit of the tree in the middle of the garden or even touch it, or we'll die." But the snake tempted the woman with his deceit, saying, "You won't die because God knows that when you eat that fruit you will be like God, knowing good and evil." The woman looked at the beautiful tree and saw that it had good fruit. She thought about what the snake said and decided the tree would make her wise, so she took some of the fruit and ate it. She also gave some of it to her husband to eat. At that moment they suddenly realized they were naked, and they sewed fig leaves together for clothes.

That evening they heard the Lord God walking in the garden, but they hid from him. The Lord God called out, "Where are you?" Adam answered, "I heard you in the garden, but I was afraid because I was naked, so I hid myself." God asked, "Who told you you were naked? Did you eat from the tree I commanded you not to?" Adam blamed the woman, whom he had named Eve, saying, "The woman you created to be with me gave me fruit from that tree and I ate it." So God asked the woman, "What have you done?" The woman blamed the snake, saying, "The snake tricked me and I ate the fruit."

God was angry and declared there would be consequences for what they did. The snake had to crawl on its belly and eat dust all its life. God also made the snake, the woman, and their offspring hate one another, striking out at one another forever. The woman, who wanted to have children with her husband, would have great pain during childbirth. As for the man, because he ate the fruit offered by the woman, he would have to work hard until the day he died to make the ground produce enough food to eat. The Lord then drove them out of the garden of Eden.

Cain Murders Abel
(Genesis 4)

Adam and Eve had two sons. They named the first son Cain and the second son Abel. Cain was a farmer, and Abel was a shepherd. One day they both brought offerings to the Lord. Cain brought an offering from his harvest and Abel brought a lamb born to his best sheep. God was pleased with Abel's offering, but rejected Cain's. This made Cain very angry. But the Lord said to him, "Why do you look so angry?" He told Cain that if he would do well, he would be accepted, but if not, sin would be at his door.

Cain was so angry that he killed Abel. The Lord asked Cain where Abel was, but Cain answered, "I don't know. Do I have to take care of my brother?" Then the Lord asked Cain, "What did you do? I hear your brother's spilled blood crying out to me from the ground." The Lord was so angry at what Cain had done that he said to Cain, "Now you are cursed. You can't farm the land anymore. If you try to grow crops, nothing will grow. You will be a fugitive and wander around from place to place." Then Cain went away from the presence of the Lord. He left Eden and lived in Nod, which is east of Eden.

Adam's Descendants to Noah and His Sons
(Genesis 5)

God gave Adam and Eve another son to replace Abel. They named him Seth. Seth and his descendants feared the Lord and tried to obey him, but they were not innocent. Everyone sins. One of Seth's descendants was Methuselah, who lived to be 969, the oldest man who ever lived. Methuselah had many grandchildren; one of them was named Noah.

The Great Flood
(Genesis 6–9)

The population of the earth kept increasing, but the Lord saw that many people were wicked and that they were always thinking evil thoughts. The Lord began to be sorry hat he had made humans at all. He regretted it so much that he decided to wipe out not only the people but also everything else he created. But God was happy with Noah.

So God said to Noah, "I have decided to destroy all people because of their evil deeds. Make yourself an ark because I'm going to flood the earth to destroy everything on it. But I'm making a promise to you, Noah; you will come into the ark with your wife, your sons, and your sons' wives. You should also bring two of every kind of animal into the ark, one male and one female."

So Noah built the ark and went into it with his family and two of every animal. Then God caused rain to fall for forty days and forty nights, and the water got so deep it covered the highest mountains. Every living thing on earth died. But Noah, his family, and the animals in the ark were spared.

God didn't forget about Noah. God caused a wind to blow over the earth and the water started going down. For months the wind blew and the water went down, until the ark finally came to rest on a mountain. Noah sent a dove out of the ark but the water wasn't gone so the dove didn't find anything to rest on and returned to the ark. After waiting seven days, Noah let the dove fly out again, and in the evening it came back with a fresh olive leaf in its mouth. Noah knew the water had gone down some. After waiting another seven days, he again sent out the dove; but it did not return. Noah knew that the earth must finally be dry. So, Noah left the ark and brought an offering to the Lord to thank him. This pleased the Lord and he said, "In the future I won't ever curse the earth because of what people think and do. I know they think evil thoughts from the time they are young, but I'll never again destroy every living creature with water as I just did." And God put a rainbow in the clouds as a sign that he would keep his promise.

The Tower of Babel
(Genesis 11)

At this time, everyone on the whole earth spoke the same language. The people decided to build a city with a tower that reached up to heaven. They were trying to make a name for themselves. But the Lord came down to see the city and said, "Speaking the same language, these people will be able to do anything they want. This is just the beginning." So he made them speak different languages, and they didn't understand one another anymore. Then the Lord scattered the people all over the earth, so they had to quit building the tower. From that time, that place was called Babel, which means 'confusion.'

The Founding of Israel

The Call of Abraham
(Genesis 12–13)

Terah, a grandson of Shem's, lived in Mesopotamia with his three sons, Abraham, Nahor, and Haran. The Lord said to Abraham, "Leave your country, your relatives, and your father's house to go to the land that I will show you." So Abraham took his wife Sarah and their nephew Lot and went to Canaan. Then the Lord appeared to Abraham and said, "I will give this land to your descendants." So Abraham built an altar to the Lord at the place where the Lord had appeared to him.

Now Abraham was very rich. He had a lot of livestock, silver, and gold. His nephew Lot also had many sheep and cattle. Together they had so many animals that there wasn't enough land for them to graze on, which made Lot's and Abraham's herdsmen quarrel over the pastures. So Abraham said to Lot, "We're family, so let's not argue. If you will take the land on the left side, then I will take the land on the right; or, if you go to the right side, then I will go to the left." Lot chose the whole plain of Jordan and settled toward the east, near Sodom. But the people of Sodom were wicked and sinned against the Lord.

Lot's Captivity and Rescue
(Genesis 14)

Four kings went to war against the kings of Sodom and Gomorrah. The kings won the battle and took everything from the two cities. They also took Lot and all he owned and left the area.

When Abraham heard that his nephew was captured, he gathered 318 of his servants and pursued the enemy. Having overtaken them, he brought back all the property and set Lot and his people free. When Abraham returned, Melchizedek, king of Salem [sometimes identified with Jerusalem] and the priest of the Most High God, came out to meet him. Melchizedek blessed Abraham and brought him bread and wine. And the king of Salem said to Abraham, "Keep the property you recovered, but give me the people." Abraham answered, "I will not take so much as a thread or a sandal-strap or anything that is yours; then you can never say, 'I made Abraham rich.'"

God's Covenant with Abraham
(Genesis 15:5–6; 18:1–14)

The Lord appeared again to Abraham in a vision and promised as many descendants as there are stars. But Abraham and Sarah were now both old, and they had no children. Nevertheless, Abraham believed the Lord, and the Lord was pleased at Abraham's faith.

One day Abraham was sitting at the door of his tent during the hottest part of the day. He looked up and saw three men coming toward him. He ran out to meet them, bowed to the ground before them, and said, "Please don't pass by my house without stopping, but rest here under this tree. I will get some water to wash your feet and food for you to eat. Then, you can continue on your way." And they answered, "Thank you, we accept."

So Abraham ran to his herd and had a fine calf killed and prepared for eating. Sarah made cakes from flour. Abraham took some cream and other food and set it all before the men. He stood by them under the tree while they ate. Then one of them said, "Where is your wife, Sarah?" Abraham answered, "She is in the tent." And he said, "Nine months from now I will return, and Sarah will have a son." Sarah, who was in the tent, heard this and laughed because she was too old to bear children. But the Lord said, "Why did Sarah laugh? Is anything impossible with the Lord?"

Judgment Pronounced on Sodom
(Genesis 18:16–33)

The men who were visiting Abraham and Sarah got up to leave and Abraham went with them. Then the Lord decided to tell Abraham his plan and said, "I will destroy Sodom, for its sin is great." The men went on to Sodom, and Abraham stood alone before the Lord and said, "Will you also destroy the righteous with the wicked? If there are fifty righteous people in the city would you spare the city for their sake?" The Lord answered, "If I find fifty righteous ones, I will spare the city." Abraham said, "If there are forty-five, would you destroy the whole city because there are five too few?" The Lord said, "If I find forty-five, I will not destroy it." Abraham went on praying until he came down to ten, and the Lord still promised to spare the city if only ten righteous people could be found in it.

Meanwhile, the men, who were angels, arrived at Sodom and stayed in Lot's house. Then the men of Sodom surrounded the house and demanded the men be brought to them. But the angels struck the wicked men with blindness and brought Lot and his wife and his two daughters out of the city. One of the angels said, "Don't look back and don't stop in the valley, but escape to the mountain." But Lot's wife looked back and turned into a pillar of salt. Then the Lord burned Sodom and Gomorrah, and the fertile plain where the two cities once stood was changed into the Dead Sea. There were not even ten righteous people in the city.

Isaac's Birth and the Command to Sacrifice Isaac
(Genesis 21–22)

The Lord blessed Sarah and Abraham with a child even though Abraham was 100 years old. They called the child Isaac. Several years after Isaac's birth, God tested Abraham. He said, "Take your only son Isaac, whom you love so much, and go to the land of Moriah. When you get there, sacrifice him on the mountain which I will show you." So, Abraham got up early the next morning, saddled his donkey, and took Isaac and two of his servants with him. Abraham took wood for the sacrifice and went to the place God had told him about. On the third day Abraham saw the place in the distance and said to his servants, "Stay here, while the boy and I go and worship." He took the wood for the offering and had Isaac carry it. Then Isaac asked, "Where is the lamb for the sacrifice?" Abraham answered, "God himself will provide that, son."

When they came to the place, Abraham built an altar, laid the wood on it, and tied up Isaac and laid him on the wood. Then he picked up a knife to kill Isaac. But the Lord called to him from heaven saying, "Abraham, Abraham, don't hurt your son. Now I know that you fear God because you have not withheld your only son from me." Then Abraham looked up and saw a ram caught in a bush by his horns. And he took the ram and offered him for a burnt offering in place of his son.

The Lord spoke to Abraham from heaven a second time and said, "Because you have not withheld your only son, I will greatly bless you and give you as many descendants as there are stars in heaven or grains of sand upon the seashore. And from your descendants, all of the nations shall be blessed."

Abraham went back to where he had left his servants and they went home together.

Isaac
(Genesis 14; 25:1–11)

After Sarah's death, Abraham said to his oldest servant, Eliezer, "Promise me that you will not choose a wife for Isaac from the women in Canaan. Instead, go back to the country where I was born and get a wife for my son from among my relatives." So, Eliezer took ten of his master's camels with him and went to Mesopotamia to the city of Nahor, Abraham's homeland. In the evening when the women came to draw water, he made his camels kneel down by a well near the city. He prayed, "O God of Abraham, show kindness to my master on this day. As I stand here by the well where young women draw water, I will say to one of them, 'Let me drink water from your pitcher.' I pray that if she says, 'Yes, and I will give some water to your camels, too,' let her be the one whom you have appointed as a wife for your servant Isaac."

Before he had finished speaking, a pretty young woman came near with a pitcher on her shoulder and went down to the well to fill it. Eliezer ran to meet her, and said, "Please give me a drink of water." She said, "Please have a drink and I will draw some water for your camels, too." When she had finished, he gave her a ring and two bracelets of gold and asked, "Whose daughter are you?" She said, "I am Rebekah, the daughter of Bethuel, the son of Nahor." Then the man bowed his head and worshiped the Lord and said, "Blessed be the Lord who has led me straight to the house of my master's relatives."

Laban, the brother of Rebekah, went out to meet Abraham's servant and led him to Bethuel's house to get something to eat. But Eliezer would not eat until he had explained his mission. When he had told them, Laban and Bethuel said, "This is from the Lord, so there is no decision to make. Take Rebekah and let her be the wife of your master's son." So the servant took Rebekah and went back to Canaan. After the servant told Isaac everything he had done, Isaac brought Rebekah into the tent that Sarah had lived in. Rebekah became his wife and he loved her.

Abraham lived his life in the faith of God's promises. He died at the age of 175. Isaac inherited all that his father had and became the chief of his people. The Lord blessed him and said, "I will give the land of Canaan to you and your descendants and through you all the nations of the earth shall be blessed."

Esau and Jacob
(Genesis 25:19–34)

Twenty years had passed and Rebekah was still childless. Then the Lord said to her, "You shall bear two sons and the older one shall serve the younger one." And she gave birth to twins. The first-born was hairy all over and was called Esau. The second was called Jacob. When the boys grew older, Esau became a skillful hunter but Jacob was a quiet man, staying near the tents. Esau was his father Isaac's favorite, and Jacob was his mother Rebekah's favorite.

One day, after Jacob had cooked some soup, Esau came home from the field tired and extremely hungry. Esau said to him, "Give me some soup." Jacob responded by saying, "I will, if you will give me your rights as the first-born son." Esau said, "I'm so hungry I could die; what good will my birthright do me?" So Esau gave up his birthright to Jacob for some soup. Esau ate and drank and went on his way, thus showing contempt for his birthright.

Jacob Obtains His Father's Blessing
(Genesis 27)

Isaac grew old and became blind. One day he sent for his older son, Esau, and said to him, "You know I'm old. Take your bow and arrows and go hunting, so you can prepare a special meal for me. I will eat it and then bless you before I die." Having overheard this conversation, Isaac's wife Rebekah told their younger son Jacob to go to his father instead of Esau so that Jacob would be the one blessed. But Jacob said, "Mother, you know that Esau's arms are hairy and mine aren't. What if father touches me and realizes that I am deceiving him? If that happens I'll be cursed, not blessed."

But she told him to do as she said. So Jacob got two goats, and Rebekah made a meal for Isaac. Then she dressed Jacob in his brother Esau's best clothes. Next, she put the goat skins on Jacob's hands and neck. Jacob took the meal to his father and asked him for the blessing.

But Isaac asked, "How did you finish hunting so quickly, son?" "The Lord helped me," answered Jacob. Isaac thought something was strange so he asked his son to come closer to him. Jacob moved nearer to his father, who touched him and said, "Sounds like Jacob but the arms feel like Esau's." So, Isaac ate the meal which Jacob had brought him and then he blessed Jacob, thus making him the one to rule over his older brother, Esau.

Jacob had just left his father when Esau returned from hunting. Esau made his father a meal and brought it to him. "Sit up, father, and eat this meal I prepared for you. Then you can bless me," said Esau. But Isaac said, "Who are you?" Esau answered, "I am your first-born son, Esau." When he heard this Isaac began to tremble all over, and he asked, "Who was it, then, who just brought me a meal? I ate it just before you came. Whoever it was, I gave him my final blessing, and so it is his forever." Realizing what had happened, Esau hated Jacob because Jacob had cheated him out of his father's blessing. He threatened to kill Jacob after his father's death. Therefore, Rebekah said to Jacob, "Go stay with Laban, my brother, until your brother's anger subsides."

Jacob Journeys to Laban
(Genesis 28–31)

Jacob left home and found a place to spend the night. He dreamt that a ladder was set up on the earth that reached all the way to heaven. Angels of God were going up and down the ladder. And the Lord was there standing beside him saying, "I am the God of Abraham and the God of Isaac. I will give you the land where you are sleeping. And your descendants will be as many as there are particles of dust on the earth. Through you and your descendants, all the nations will be blessed. I will always be with you and I will bring you back to this place." Jacob answered, "What a terrifying place! It must be the house of God; it must be the gate that opens into heaven." The next morning Jacob made a memorial at this spot.

Jacob then traveled to the east to his uncle Laban's, where he stayed and worked for a month. Laban asked Jacob, "What can I pay you for your work?" Now Laban had two daughters, Leah and her younger sister, Rachel, who was very beautiful. Jacob said, "I will work for you for seven years if I can marry Rachel." Laban agreed and the time passed by quickly because Jacob loved Rachel. But when the seven years were completed, Laban gave Jacob Leah instead, saying, "It is not the custom here that the younger daughter be married before the older." Thus, Jacob married Leah.

So, Jacob had to serve seven more years for Rachel. After Jacob and Rachel were married, Jacob worked seven more years. This time he was paid for his work. Jacob then went back to the land of Canaan with his wives Leah and Rachel, their children, and all that he had.

Jacob Meets Esau
(Genesis 32–33; 35:25–29)

When Jacob neared Canaan, he sent messengers ahead to his brother Esau so that things might go well between them. The messengers returned and told Jacob, "Your brother is coming to meet you, and he has 400 men with him." Jacob was afraid, so he sent Esau a gift from his flocks and herds and prayed to the Lord for help. The Lord appeared to Jacob as a man and wrestled with him. Jacob wouldn't let the man go until he blessed Jacob. And the Lord blessed him, and changed his name from Jacob to Israel, which means "one who struggles with God."

When Jacob saw Esau, he bowed before him seven times. But Esau ran to meet him and hugged and kissed him and they both cried for joy. Their father Isaac died at the age of 180 years. And Esau and Jacob buried him.

Joseph Sold by His Brothers
(Genesis 37)

Jacob had twelve sons, but he loved Joseph more than his other sons. Out of this love, Jacob made Joseph a special coat with sleeves. Joseph's brothers were envious that their father loved him more than them, so they hated Joseph. Joseph told his father about his brothers' bad behavior.

One night Joseph had a dream and he told it to his brothers. "We were tying bundles of grain in the fields," Joseph said, "and your bundles bowed down to mine." In another dream, Joseph saw the sun, the moon, and eleven stars bow down to him. But his brothers were angry and protested, "You think that you are going to rule over us!" And so his brothers hated Joseph all the more. Joseph's father, Jacob, also criticized Joseph and said, "What is this dream? Will your mother and I and your brothers all bow down to you?" Still, Jacob kept the dream in mind.

One day Jacob's other sons were watching the flocks far away from home so Jacob said to Joseph, "Go and see if things are going well for your brothers and then come back and tell me." When the brothers saw Joseph from a distance they said, "Here comes the dreamer. Let's kill him and see what will become of his dreams!" But Reuben, Jacob's oldest son, wanted to save Joseph and said, "Don't harm him. Let's throw him into this pit instead." When Joseph arrived they tore off his special coat and threw him into an empty pit that had no water.

Then, as Joseph's brothers sat down to eat, some merchants came by on their way to Egypt to sell their goods. Judah, one of the brothers, said to the others, "Let's sell Joseph to those merchants instead of hurting him. After all, he is our brother." So they sold Joseph for twenty pieces of silver and he was taken to Egypt by the merchants.

Reuben was away from the group when this happened and when he returned he said, "Joseph is gone!" After the others told Reuben what had happened, they decided to kill a goat, dip Joseph's coat in the blood, and bring the coat to their father. Returning home, they said to Jacob, "We have found this coat. Isn't this the coat you gave to Joseph?" And Jacob recognized the coat and said, "This is his coat. A wild beast has devoured him!" Even though all his sons and daughters tried to comfort him, Jacob would not be consoled. He grieved for his son many days.

Joseph Thrown into Prison
(Genesis 39)

The merchants who now owned Joseph took him to Egypt where they sold him to the captain of Pharaoh's army. But God was with Joseph and protected him. The captain made Joseph chief servant of his house. Joseph, however, was a very handsome man, so the captain's wife tried to seduce him. But he refused her advances and said, "How can I sin against God?" Out of anger, she falsely accused him of assaulting her. Her husband believed her and put Joseph in prison.

But even there, the Lord was with Joseph and saw to it that he was favored by the prison guard. As a result, the guard gave Joseph the responsibility of caring for all the other prisoners.

Joseph Interprets Dreams
(Genesis 40–41)

Pharaoh was angry with both his chief butler and chief baker, so they were put into the same prison as Joseph. One morning, when Joseph talked to them he saw they were very sad. When Joseph asked why, they said they both had dreams but there was no one to help them interpret the dreams. Joseph asked that they tell him the dreams. The butler said, "I dreamed that I saw a vine with three branches. I pressed juice out of the grapes, poured the juice into Pharaoh's cup and gave it to him." Joseph said, "Within three days you shall be restored to your position in Pharaoh's house. When this happens, please remember me and mention to Pharaoh that I have done nothing to deserve imprisonment." Then the baker told Joseph about his dream. He said, "I had three baskets on my head, and the basket on top was full of baked food for Pharaoh, but the birds came and ate it." Joseph said, "Within three days Pharaoh will behead you." It all happened just as Joseph had predicted, but the butler forgot about Joseph.

Two years later Pharaoh dreamed that he was standing by the Nile River. Seven fat cows came up out of the river and grazed on the bank. After this, seven lean cows came. out of the river and devoured the fat ones. Then he dreamed that seven full ears of corn grew on one stalk, but seven thin ears grew next to them and consumed the full ears of corn. None of the wise men of Egypt could interpret Pharaoh's dreams. Then the butler remembered Joseph and Pharaoh sent for him. Pharaoh said to Joseph, "I have heard that as soon as I tell you my dream you can interpret it." And Joseph answered, "It is not me, but God who will provide a good interpretation." When Joseph heard the dreams, he gave this interpretation: "There will be seven years of plentiful harvests followed by seven years of famine. The years of famine will consume all that was extra in the years of plenty." When the king heard the interpretation, he appointed Joseph minister of agriculture over all of Egypt and Joseph went from place to place storing up grain during the years of plenty.

Joseph's Brothers Go to Egypt
(Genesis 42–44)

As Joseph had predicted, a famine came upon all the lands, but in Egypt grain was still stored up. So Jacob sent ten of his sons to Egypt to buy grain. Jacob kept Benjamin, the youngest, at home because he was afraid that Benjamin might be harmed on the trip. When the other brothers got to Egypt, they went to Joseph, who was now the governor, and bowed down before him, but did not recognize him. Joseph, however, did recognize them and remembered his dreams about them. They told Joseph that there were twelve brothers, but that the youngest was at home with their father, and that one brother was dead. Joseph said to them, "You are spies," and he put them in prison for three days. On the third day said to them, "One of you must stay in prison but the others may go home with the grain. And bring your youngest brother back here to prove that you are speaking the truth." Then they said to one another, "This crisis happened because of what we did to Joseph." Overhearing them, Joseph turned away and wept. Then, he picked his brother Simeon to remain in prison and had him bound, while he allowed the others to return home to the land of Canaan.

Joseph Makes Himself Known
(Genesis 45)

When his brothers returned with Benjamin, Joseph was able to control himself no longer. He cried to his brothers, "I am Joseph! Is my father still alive?" But they couldn't answer because they were so afraid of him. Still, Joseph spoke to them with kindness. He kissed them and cried as he hugged his brother Benjamin. Then he said,

"Hurry back to father and tell him that I am ruler over all of Egypt. Bring him here." And they went home and told Jacob all these things, but Jacob didn't believe them. Then he saw the wagons which Joseph had sent to bring him to Egypt, and said, "My son, Joseph, is still alive. I must go and see him before I die."

Jacob Goes Down to Egypt
(Genesis 46–50)

The Lord spoke to Jacob in a vision and said, "Do not be afraid to go down to Egypt. I will be with you and bring you back again. Joseph will be with you when you die." Jacob went to Egypt with his whole family, which numbered seventy people. When Joseph heard that his father was near, he got his chariot ready and went to meet him in the land of Goshen. As soon as Joseph saw Jacob he fell into his father's arms and wept a long time. Jacob said, "Now I can die, since I have seen that you are still alive." When Joseph told Pharaoh that his family had arrived, Pharaoh told Joseph to give his father and his family the land of Goshen to live in. This was land fit for shepherds because of its good pastures.

Jacob lived seventeen years in Egypt and reached the age of 147 before he died. Joseph took his father's body back to Canaan and buried it in the tomb with Jacob's ancestors, Abraham and Isaac.

Joseph's brothers feared that he would now take vengeance on them, but Joseph wept when he heard of their fears. He said to them, "Am I capable of taking the place of God? You intended to harm me, but God intended me to live in order to keep many people alive."

The Exodus and Conquest of Canaan
Birth of Moses
(Exodus 1–2:1–10)

The Israelites, who were called Hebrews, lived in Egypt for over four centuries and multiplied until there were many descendants of Joseph. By then another Pharaoh ruled over Egypt who didn't know anything about Joseph's legacy. He said to his people, "We are in danger because there are so many Israelites, and they are more powerful than we are." So King Pharaoh oppressed them with hard work, to try to keep them from multiplying, but their numbers increased anyway. Next the king declared that every son born to Hebrew women should be killed; only the daughters would be allowed to live.

About this time a Hebrew woman of the tribe of Levi had a son, and seeing that he was a beautiful child, hid him for three months. When she couldn't hide him any longer, she made a waterproof basket out of reeds, put the child in it, and laid it in the tall weeds at the edge of the Nile. The baby's sister stood above the river to see what would happen to him. Soon the daughter of King Pharaoh came down to the river to bathe. Seeing the basket, she asked her maid to bring it to her. When she opened it, the baby was crying, and the princess had compassion for him. The baby's sister then came down and asked, "Shall I call a nurse?" Pharaoh's daughter answered, "Yes." So the sister went and got her and her brother's own mother. When he was grown, his mother brought him back to the princess, who named him Moses, which means 'he that is drawn out of the water.'

Moses in Midian
(Exodus 2:11–3:4)

When Moses was forty years old, he went out and saw how hard his fellow Hebrews were forced to work. He also saw an Egyptian strike an Israelite. Moses looked all around and, seeing no one, he killed the Egyptian and buried him in the sand. When Pharaoh heard about it, he sought to kill Moses. But Moses fled to Midian, and tended the flock of his father-in-law, Jethro, who was a priest there. Moses stayed in Midian forty years.

Once, while he was watching the flocks at Mount Horeb, he saw a bush on fire that did not burn up. When he was about to get closer to it, the Lord called to him from the bush, and said, "Take off your shoes; the place where you are standing is holy ground. I am the God of Abraham, Isaac, and Jacob. I have seen the misery of my people in Egypt and have heard their cry. Therefore, I will send you to Pharaoh, so you may bring my people out of Egypt." Moses answered, "What if they do not believe you sent me?" Then the Lord said, "Throw your shepherd's staff on the ground." When Moses did, it became a serpent, and Moses stepped back from it. Then the Lord told Moses to lift the snake by the tail; when he did so, it became a rod again.

The Lord also gave Moses power to work other miracles. But Moses continued to make excuses why he shouldn't be the one to go to Pharaoh. He even said that he was not capable of speaking in public. But the Lord answered, "I will send your brother Aaron with you. You can tell him what to say, and he will speak for you." Then Moses went to Egypt. The Lord sent Aaron to meet him and they went together to tell the Israelites what the Lord had said, and they all rejoiced and worshiped the Lord.

The Exodus
(Exodus 5–14)

Moses and Aaron went to Pharaoh and said, "The Lord God of Israel says, 'Let my people go." But Pharaoh answered, "Who is this Lord? Why should I do what he says? I don't know him and I will not let the Israelites go." Instead, he made them work harder.

Even though Moses performed the miracles that the Lord had shown him, Pharaoh's heart remained hard, and he would not let the people go. So God said to Moses, "Stretch your hand out over the Nile." When Moses did so, the water of the Nile became blood. When this still did not persuade Pharaoh, the Lord sent nine other plagues over Egypt, including frogs, gnats, flies, and disease. The eighth plague consisted of countless locusts that covered the land and ate everything that was green. The ninth was a thick darkness that lasted for three days. But in Goshen, where the Israelites lived, there were no locusts and there was no darkness.

Finally, the Lord told Moses to say to the children of Israel, "To-night you shall kill a lamb in every house and sprinkle the blood on the door posts; you shall roast the lamb and eat it with unleavened bread and bitter herbs, standing with your sandals on your feet, ready to go." This was how the Lord instituted the first Passover.

At midnight the Lord passed through Egypt and slew the first-born of every Egyptian, from that of Pharaoh to that of the slaves; but he saw the lamb's blood on the houses of the Israelites and passed over them, sparing their children. Then there was a loud cry in all Egypt because there was death in every home. Pharaoh now decided to let the Israelites leave Egypt. Thus, about 600,000 men, women, and children fled Egypt, with the Lord leading them as a pillar of fire by night and a pillar of cloud by day, toward the Red Sea.

Now Pharaoh changed his mind about letting the people of Israel go and pursued them with all his war-chariots, overtaking them at the Red Sea. When the Israelites saw Pharaoh's men coming, they complained to Moses, saying, "Weren't there enough graves in Egypt? Did you have to take us out to the wilderness to die?" But he answered, "Don't be afraid. Stand still and see how the Lord will save you." Then Moses stretched out his hand, and the Red Sea divided so that the Israelites could walk on dry ground, with a wall of water on both the right and left of them. Pharaoh pursued them into the Red Sea, but when the Israelites had crossed to the other side, Moses stretched out his hand again; and the waters returned, drowning Pharaoh's army.

Wandering in the Wilderness
(Exodus; Numbers; Deuteronomy)

The Israelites traveled into the Sinai desert, but they could find no water or food there, so they complained to Moses that they wished they were back in Egypt. Moses cried out to the Lord, who told him to strike a rock with his rod, and water flowed out of it. Then the people complained that they had no food, so the Lord sent them manna, which is like bread, raining down from heaven and lying every morning like frost on the ground and melting when the sun rose.

Three months after they had left Egypt, they camped near Mount Sinai. On the morning of their third day there, there was a thick cloud on the mountain. The thunder and lightning in the cloud were so powerful that the people trembled. The Lord said to Moses, "Come up to me on the mountain, and I will give you stone tablets with the

Law written on them." So Moses climbed the mountain and the Lord gave him the two tablets of the Law. But while Moses was on the mountain, the people said to Aaron, "Make us a god to lead us because Moses has not returned." So Aaron made a golden calf, and the people danced around it. When Moses came down from the mountain and saw the calf, he became angry and threw the stone tablets against the mountain so hard that they broke. He took the golden calf, ground it to powder, and threw it in the brook which ran down the side of the mountain. Then he told the Levites, men who belonged to the tribe of Levi, to go through the camp with their swords drawn; 3,000 people were killed with those swords.

Moses went back up the mountain and stayed there forty days and forty nights. During that time he didn't eat or drink. And the Lord wrote the Ten Commandments [quoted below from the New Revised Standard Version (NRSV) Bible] on two new tables of stone which, from that time on, were kept in a chest overlaid with gold, called the Ark of the Covenant.

1. "You shall have no other gods before me."
2. "You shall not make wrongful use of the name of the Lord your God. ."
3. "Remember the Sabbath day, and keep it holy."
4. "Honor your father and your mother. ."
5. "You shall not murder."
6. "You shall not commit adultery."
7. "You shall not steal."
8. "You shall not bear false witness against your neighbor."
9. "You shall not covet your neighbor's house. ."
10. ". . . you shall not covet your neighbor's wife, or male or female slave, or ox, or donkey, or anything that belongs to your neighbor."

The Lord commanded Moses to give the people laws concerning worship, too, and he made Aaron high priest. Aaron's sons became priests as well, and the Levites were made their assistants.

A tabernacle, or large tent, was built as a place of worship. It was divided into two parts: the Holy Place and the Most Holy Place [also known as the Holy of Holies]. In the Holy of Holies there were the Ark of the Covenant and a golden pot filled with manna. No one except the high priest was allowed to go in the Holy of Holies, and he could do so only once each year. The other part, the Holy Place, was for the priests. Around the tabernacle there was a roofless court where the people gathered.

The seventh day of the week was called the Sabbath, which means 'day of rest.' Three great feasts were celebrated: (1) the Passover, to commemorate the deliverance out of Egypt, (2) the Feast of Weeks [or Pentecost], and (3) the Feast of Tabernacles.

Several kinds of sacrifices were made at the tabernacle, but the most important one was made on the Day of Atonement [now known in Judaism as Yom Kippur], when the high priest entered the Holy of Holies and offered the blood of an ox and a male goat for his own sins and the sins of the people.

Now the Israelites moved on from Sinai toward Canaan. Moses sent spies on ahead who returned, saying, "The land is excellent, but we're like grasshoppers compared with the people there; they are so big!" But two of the spies, Joshua and Caleb, said, "We can conquer the land, for the Lord is with us." But it was no use; the people refused even to try to fight the Canaanites.

So they wandered about in the wilderness, where it was very dry and there were snakes. But the Lord sustained them so that their clothes didn't get old and their feet didn't swell. Still, they often grumbled about the Lord and provoked him. One day they complained that they needed food and water, but the Lord sent venomous snakes among them instead, which bit the people, killing many of them. Finally, the people humbled themselves, and Moses prayed for them. And the Lord said, "Make a snake of brass and put it on a pole." And whoever had been bitten but looked up at the snake of brass, lived.

After the forty years had passed, the Israelites drew near the land of Canaan. Only the Jordan River separated them from that land of promise. Then Moses climbed the mountain of Nebo, and the Lord showed him all the land. God said, "This is the land that I promised to Abraham, Isaac, Jacob, and their descendants, but you will not go through the river to it." So Moses, the Lord's servant, died there at the age of 120 and the Lord buried him. Never again was there a prophet in Israel with whom the Lord spoke face-to-face, as he had done with Moses.

Joshua
(Joshua)

The Lord appointed Joshua prophet after Moses died, saying to him, "Just as I was with Moses, I will also be with you." After mourning the death of Moses for thirty days, the Israelites prepared to cross the Jordan River. The priests carried the Ark of the Covenant ahead of the people. As soon as the priests' feet touched the water of the Jordan, the water parted so that the people passed through on dry ground. The manna the Lord had been providing stopped falling and they ate the fruit of the land.

Jericho was a fortified town that the Israelites were able to take over without resistance. The priests and all the armed men walked around the city once a day for six days. On the seventh day they marched around it seven times. Then the priests blew trumpets, the people shouted, the walls fell, and Jericho was conquered. In seven years, Joshua conquered thirty-one kings, and he divided their land among the twelve tribes of Israel. After many years Joshua gathered those tribes, and said, "Choose today whom you will serve: the Lord or the gods of the heathens. But as for me and my house, we will serve the Lord." The people answered, "We will serve the Lord and obey his voice." Joshua lived to be 110 years old.

The Time of the Judges
Deborah, Gideon, and Samson
(Judges)

The Israelites did serve the Lord while Joshua was alive, but after his death they turned away from the Lord, married the daughters of the Canaanites, and served false gods. So the Lord, angry with the people, delivered them into the hands of heathens. But the people cried to the Lord, so he provided judges to save them.

One of these judges was Deborah, a prophetess. Deborah led an army of 10,000 men in battle against King Jabin of Canaan. On the day of victory over the Canaanites, she sang this song of praise: "When the people give themselves willingly to the Lord, thanks be to God! Kings and princes, listen to this song. I sing praises to the Lord God of Israel."

Then Midianites threatened Israel with war. An angel of the Lord came to Gideon, another of the judges, as he was threshing wheat, and called upon him to save the people. So Gideon sent messengers to the tribes and an army of 32,000 men gathered around him. But the Lord said, "There are too many of you. Israel might become filled with pride saying, 'We saved ourselves.' Therefore, go tell the army that whoever is afraid of battle may return home." So 22,000 of them went away; 10,000 remained. But the Lord said, "There are still too many people. Choose 300 men." Then Gideon chose 300 men and divided them into three companies. He gave each man a trumpet and an empty pitcher with a torch in it. At midnight they went down to the Midianites' camp, broke their pitchers, held up the torches, and blew their trumpets. The Midianites fled and were chased in battle by Gideon and his men.

When the Philistines oppressed the Israelites, the Lord sent the judge Samson as their deliverer. He overcame the enemy time and again because the Lord had given him great strength. In fact, Samson had so much strength that he once killed a young lion with his bare hands. Nevertheless, Samson allowed Delilah to trick him. She shaved off his long locks of hair, which were the source of his strength, and delivered him over to the Philistines. They blinded Samson and made him grind corn in the prison house. Having gathered in the temple of their god Dagon for a great feast, the Philistines brought Samson out to make fun of him. But by now his hair had grown back and his strength had returned. Samson prayed to the Lord, took hold of the two middle pillars which held up the temple, and pulled them down so that the temple fell and buried both Samson and his enemies.

Ruth
(Ruth)

During the period when the judges ruled, there was a famine in the land. At that time, a man traveled from Bethlehem to the country of Moab with his wife Naomi and two sons. But he died, and Naomi's sons married Orpah and Ruth, who were Moabites. After ten years, the sons also died, and Naomi prepared to return to the land of Israel along with Orpah and Ruth. But on the way, Naomi said to them, "Return to Moab my daughters. May the Lord be kind to you, as you have been to me." Orpah did return to Moab, but Ruth said to her mother-in-law, "Your people shall be my people and your God my God. Only death will separate us." So Naomi and Ruth continued on their way to Israel.

When they were hungry, Ruth went to get bits of grain that had fallen in a field which belonged to a rich man named Boaz. Hearing that one of these women was Ruth and that she had come with her mother-in-law, he said to the reapers, "Let some handfuls of grain fall on purpose, so that she can pick it up." Then Boaz said to Ruth, "If you are thirsty, come and drink. If you are hungry, come and eat my bread." She asked, "Why am I, a stranger, welcomed as your guest?" Boaz answered, "I heard what you did for your mother-in-law, how you left your own parents to come to a country you did not know. The Lord God of Israel, under whose wing you have come to trust, has given you reward for what you have done." After that year's harvest was completed, Boaz married Ruth and she bore a son who was named Obed. Obed was the father of Jesse, and Jesse was the father of David.

Eli and Samuel
(I Samuel 1–10)

In the time of the judges, Eli was high priest and judge. Hannah, who lived in the area ruled by Eli, prayed that she and her husband would have a child. When Eli heard her request, he, too, asked God to grant it. Hannah's prayer was answered, and she had a son, Samuel. Out of gratitude to the Lord, Hannah brought Samuel to be raised by Eli. (Eli himself had two sons who were very wicked, but he did not discipline them.)

One night, when Samuel was still young, he heard a voice call to him in his sleep. Samuel thought it was Eli who called him, but Eli said, "I did not call you. Go back to bed." It was actually the Lord who had called Samuel, but he didn't know it. The Lord called Samuel a second and third time and each time Samuel ran to see what Eli wanted. Then Eli realized that it was the Lord, so he said to Samuel, "If he calls you again, say, 'Speak Lord, for your servant hears you.'" So Samuel went to lay down and the Lord called to him again. This time Samuel answered as Eli had instructed. And the Lord continued, "Because Eli saw his sons act wickedly but did not discipline them, I will destroy Eli and his house."

In the morning, when Samuel told Eli what the Lord had revealed, Eli said, "He is the Lord. Let him do what is right to him."

Now the Philistines went to war against Israel and defeated them. The Israelites brought the Ark of the Covenant from the land Eli ruled to where the soldiers from Israel were camped. But they lost another battle, and the Ark was taken by the enemy. Eli, now ninety-eight years old, was worried about what would happen to the Ark. Just then, a soldier who had fled from the battle ran up to him and said, "The Philistines defeated Israel, both your sons are dead, and the Philistines took the Ark." When the Ark was mentioned, Eli fell backward, broke his neck, and died.

The Philistines brought the Ark back to their own land. But the Lord dealt harshly with them and they suffered from various diseases. They feared God and, after seven months, sent the Ark home again to Israel, along with expensive presents.

Samuel was the last of the judges. Every year he went through the land from place to place to judge Israel, and he was honored by the people. When he was old he attempted to make his two sons judges, but they did not follow in his ways. They accepted bribes and were not fair in their judgments. So, the elders of Israel came to Samuel and said, "Appoint us a king to govern us and to lead us in our battles." Samuel did not want to grant their request. But the Lord said to him, "Listen to these people. They have not rejected you, but they have rejected me that I should not reign over them." He also told

Samuel, "I will send you a man from the tribe of Benjamin and you shall anoint him to be the ruler over Israel." The man God referred to was Saul, and no one in Israel was a better person to rule than Saul.

When Saul arrived, the Lord said to Samuel, "This is the man I told you about." So, Samuel brought him into his house, took a vial of oil and poured it on Saul's head, and said, "The Lord has anointed you ruler over his people." The Spirit of God came upon Saul on that day and the Lord gave him a new heart. Then Samuel was no longer judge over Israel.

The Kingdom of Israel and Its Division
Saul
(I Samuel 11–16)

Saul was brave and victorious over his enemies, but he also disobeyed the law of the Lord. Therefore, Samuel said to Saul, "Your kingdom will not continue because you rejected the Lord, and so the Lord has rejected you." Then the Lord said to Samuel, "Go to Bethlehem and anoint David, the youngest son of Jesse, to be king after Saul."

So, Samuel went and anointed David, and the Spirit of the Lord was with David from that day on. But at the same time the Spirit of the Lord left Saul, and an evil spirit now troubled him. However, when the evil spirit bothered Saul, David would play the harp for him. When David played the harp, Saul was relieved and would feel better.

David and Goliath
(I Samuel 17)

At a time when Israel was at war with the Philistines, Goliath (a Philistine) came by the Israelite camp. Goliath was a valiant warrior who mocked the Israelites because no one dared fight him. David heard Goliath's challenge and knew that the king's daughter was promised to anyone who could kill this warrior. David said, "I was a shepherd for my father's flock and whenever a lion or a bear took a lamb I went after it, killed it, and saved the lamb. The Lord who saved me from the lion and the bear will deliver me from Goliath, too." And Saul said, "Go and the Lord will be with you."

David took his staff, sling, and five smooth stones from a brook and went to Goliath. When Goliath saw David, he said, "Am I a dog that you would come at me with stones and a sling?" David answered, "You come to me with a sword and spear, but I come to you in the name of the Lord of hosts." With that, he put a stone in his sling and threw it at Goliath, who was hit on the forehead so hard that he fell to the ground. Then David ran, drew the Philistine's sword from its sheath, and killed him. As a result, Saul made David commander over the army and gave him his daughter in marriage. And Jonathan, Saul's son, loved David like a brother.

Saul Pursues David and Saul Dies
(I Samuel 18–31; II Samuel 1)

When David returned after slaying Goliath, the women sang, "Saul has killed thousands, but David has killed tens of thousands." This made Saul angry, and from that day on he was David's enemy. Twice after that, while David played the harp for the king to try to relieve him of the evil spirit, Saul threw his javelin at David to kill him, but the spear hit the wall instead. So David fled and wandered from place to place.

Once the king went into a cave where David was hiding, but David didn't lay a hand on Saul. Instead he cut off a piece of Saul's robe, which he showed to Saul after they had left the cave. Saul wept and said, "You are more righteous than I because you were good to me even when I was evil to you." Then Saul went back to his house, but later he resumed his pursuit of David. One night, while Saul and his men were asleep, David went to his house and took Saul's spear and his jar of water. When Saul realized that David had again spared his life, he cried out, "Return, David, for I will no longer try to harm you." But David went to live in the land of the Philistines until Saul's death.

In a great battle with the Philistines, Saul was badly wounded and Jonathan was killed. Saul said to his armor-bearer, "Thrust your sword through me." But the soldier wouldn't kill the king, the Lord's anointed. So, Saul took a sword, fell on it, and died. David grieved for both Saul and Jonathan.

David Becomes King
(II Samuel 2–9)

After Saul's death, David was made king and ruled for forty years. With singing and dancing, David brought the Ark of the Covenant to Jerusalem, where he made his home. As king, he judged the people, but did so fairly. David wanted to honor Jonathan's memory, so he said to Jonathan's son, "I will return to you all the land that belonged to Saul, and you will always be welcome at my table." David overcame all his enemies in the land of Israel and became very powerful.

David's Fall
(II Samuel 11–12)

While David stayed in Jerusalem, he sent his commander Joab to battle the Ammonites. One evening, from the roof of his house, David saw Bathsheba, the beautiful wife of Uriah, while she was bathing. David sent for her and committed adultery with her. Bathsheba became pregnant, so David wrote to Joab and told him to send Uriah to the fiercest part of the baffle so that Uriah would be killed. Joab obeyed and Uriah was killed. When the time of mourning was over, David married Bathsheba and she had their son.

But what David had done angered the Lord, so the Lord sent the prophet Nathan to David. Nathan told him this story: "There were two men in one city, the one rich and the other poor. The rich man had many flocks and herds, but the poor man had only one lamb which would eat out of his hand, drink from his cup, and cuddle up to him. The lamb was like a child to him. One day a traveler came to see the rich man, but the rich man didn't want to kill one of his lambs for their meal, so he spared his own flocks and herds and took the poor man's lamb, making a meal of it for the stranger." The story made David very angry, and he said, "The man who did this deserves to die. He should replace the lamb fourfold." Then

Nathan said, "You are the man. You had Uriah killed by the sword of the Ammonites and took his wife to be your own."

David was severely grieved about what he had done and admitted his sin against the Lord. So, Nathan said to him, "The Lord has taken away your sin, and you will not die, but the son which Bathsheba bore will die." Soon the child became sick and died, and David was overcome with grief for the rest of his life.

Revolt of Absalom
(II Samuel 15–18; I Kings 1–2)

David's other son, Absalom, was the most handsome man in all of Israel. From the sole of his foot to the top of his head, there was no blemish on him. Though dearly loved by his father, Absalom wished he were king instead of David. So Absalom did what he could to steal the hearts of the people of Israel from his father.

In his efforts, Absalom formed a conspiracy with Ahithophel, David's counselor. Absalom led an army against Jerusalem, and David was compelled to flee for his life. Ahithophel then advised Absalom to pursue his father immediately; but Hushai, a friend of David, advised Absalom to wait until a large army could be gathered. The Lord, who was against Absalom, caused Ahithophel's advice to be ignored, so Ahithophel went home and hanged himself.

As a result, David himself gained time for gathering an army, which was led by Joab. As the army marched out, David told Joab, "Deal gently with my son Absalom." The army fought a great battle in a forest and Absalom was forced to flee. As he did, his head was caught in the branches of a large oak under which he passed and his horse went out from under him, leaving him hanging in the tree. Some of Joab's men ran to the place with spears and thrust them through Absalom's heart. When David heard what had happened, he wept and cried out, "O my son Absalom! I wish that I had died instead of you. O Absalom, my son, my son!" After reigning over Israel for forty years, David died and Solomon, a son of Bathsheba, was made king.

Solomon
(I Kings 3–11)

One night the Lord appeared to Solomon in a dream and said, "Ask for something and I will give it to you." Solomon then asked for an understanding mind to rule the people and for the ability to know good from bad. God was pleased with his request and granted Solomon the wisdom for which he asked. Solomon was indeed wiser than all other people. [The Biblical tradition attributes the Book of Proverbs to him due to his extraordinary reputation for wisdom. The tradition also attributes to him the Song of Songs, also know as the Song of Solomon.]

One day two women came before Solomon. The women lived in the same house, and each had given birth to a child. Sadly, one of the women rolled over in the night on top of her child and it died of suffocation. But when the woman woke up, she placed her dead child next to the other woman and took the other woman's child to her own bed. In the presence of Solomon, they argued as to who was the mother of the living child. Suddenly, Solomon said, "Bring me a sword." When the sword was brought to him he said, "Divide the child in two and give half to each one." At that, one of the women cried out, "Give her the child and do not kill him." Then Solomon said, "Give the child to this woman because she is his mother." All Israel heard the judgment and feared the king because they saw that the wisdom of God was in him.

On mount Moriah in Jerusalem, Solomon built a beautiful temple to the Lord and put the Ark of the Covenant in the part of it called the Holy of Holies. When the temple was finished, Solomon knelt down and prayed, "0 Lord, even heaven cannot contain you, much less this house that I have built! Yet hear whatever prayer we send up to you from this house. And when foreigners come to pray in this temple, hear their prayers too."

But Solomon did not remain faithful to the end. He married many heathen women who turned his heart to other gods, and he built altars to these false gods. And the people Solomon ruled complained because of their heavy taxes and other burdens.

Division of the Kingdom
(I Kings 12:1–24)

After Solomon died, all Israel came together and said to his son Rehoboam, "Your father made our lives very burdensome; make it easier and we will serve you." So, Rehoboam first consulted the old men who had advised his father. They said, "If you listen to the people today, they will serve you all your life." Next, he consulted the young men he grew up with. They told him to tell the people, "My father made your burden heavy, but I will make it even heavier. My father disciplined you with whips, but I will discipline you with scorpions." Rehoboam decided to follow the young men's advice.

When the people returned and heard what Rehoboam had to say, they were so angered that ten of the twelve tribes of Israel made Solomon's servant Jeroboam their king. For the sake of David, only the tribes of Judah and Benjamin stayed with Rehoboam. Samaria was the capital of the ten tribes, which were known as the Kingdom of Israel. Jerusalem was the capital of the two tribes, which was known as the Kingdom of Judah.

Jeroboam's Reign over Israel
(I Kings 12:25–14:20; 15:25–33)

Jeroboam was worried, "If the people go to the temple in Jerusalem to make sacrifices," he thought, "their hearts will turn again to King Rehoboam of Judah, and they might kill me." Therefore, Jeroboam made two calves of gold, and the people went to worship and make sacrifices. But the Lord warned Jeroboam, saying, "You have made yourself false gods; therefore, I will punish your house." As a result, when Jeroboam's son became king, he was killed, and the whole family of Jeroboam was destroyed. Then kings from other families ruled, but they were all wicked and worshiped false gods.

Ahab and Elijah
(I Kings 16–22; II Kings 9:30–37)

The most wicked of all the kings of Israel was Ahab, who married Jezebel, the evil daughter of the king of Sidon. Ahab built a temple for the god Baal, which made the Lord very angry. As a punishment the prophet Elijah told Ahab that there would be a three-year drought as well as a great famine in the land. But God sent Elijah to the city of Zarephath, where a poor widow was to care for him. Though the widow had nearly nothing, neither her food nor her oil ran out while Elijah was there. When the widow's son became sick and died, Elijah prayed to the Lord, and the child recovered.

After three years, God commanded Elijah to go to Ahab and tell the king to gather together the priests of Baal on Mount Carmel. The priests of Baal sacrificed a bull and called to their god all day long, but got no answer. Elijah mocked them, saying, "Cry out! Maybe your god is meditating, or perhaps he is asleep." In the evening Elijah sacrificed a bull and prayed, "Lord, let it be known today that you are God in Israel and that I am your servant." Then fire fell from heaven and consumed his sacrifice.

When the people saw this they said, "The Lord indeed is God," and they seized the priests of Baal and put them to death. Soon, the sky grew black with clouds and a heavy rain fell. Then Ahab told Jezebel everything Elijah had done, and she tried to kill Elijah, so he fled into the wilderness. But Elijah himself wished that he would die because Israel had broken the Lord's covenant. But God said to him, "Return. There are still seven thousand in Israel who have not bowed down to Baal." So, Elijah set out to return to Israel.

While Elijah journeyed, Ahab was trying to buy his neighbor's vineyard because it was located beside the king's palace. But the owner, Naboth, would not sell the vineyard because it was his family's inheritance. This so depressed Ahab that he lay down on his bed and would not eat. But his wife Jezebel said to him, "Get up, eat something, and be happy. I will get you the vineyard." Her plan was to have the city's nobles tell a lie, saying that Naboth had cursed both God and the king. The nobles did as they were told and Naboth was stoned to death because the people believed the lie about him. After Naboth was dead, Ahab took possession of the vineyard.

But the Lord sent Elijah to say to Ahab: "In the place where dogs licked up the blood of Naboth, they will also lick up your blood, Ahab, and dogs will eat Jezebel." And the Lord's sentence was carried out. Ahab was killed in battle, and his blood ran into his war-chariot. When the chariot was washed in Samaria, dogs came and licked up the blood. Many years later, Jezebel was thrown out a window and her body was eaten by dogs.

Fall of the Kingdom of Israel
(II Kings 17)

The kings and the people of Israel continued to worship false gods and did not heed the warnings of God's prophets. Their punishment finally came when the powerful king of Assyria, Shalmaneser, conquered Israel [also known as Samaria]. He imprisoned Hoshea, the last of the kings of Israel, and [in 722 B.C.] took the people of Israel into captivity in Assyria. Another Assyrian king sent foreigners to live in Samaria. These people eventually came to worship the Lord but they also continued to serve the gods from their native lands. Because they combined worship of the Lord with pagan practices, they were not considered true worshipers of God.

Kingdom of Judah Under Hezekiah and the Prophet Isaiah
(II Kings 10–20)

Judah had always been ruled by kings of the house of David, but many of them were wicked and served false gods. Still, some were righteous and served the Lord so that idolatry was not as firmly established there as it was in the Kingdom of Israel. The most pious of these kings of Judah was Hezekiah.

In the fourteenth year of King Hezekiah's reign, Sennacherib, King of Assyria, came against Jerusalem and boasted: "Do you think that your God can deliver you? Have the gods of other nations ever recaptured their lands from the king of Assyria?" When Hezekiah heard this, he went into the house of God to pray for deliverance. Isaiah the prophet sent word to Hezekiah that the Lord had heard his prayer. Hezekiah's prayer was answered by an angel of the Lord passing through the Assyrian's camp, slaying 185,000 in one night. So, King Sennacherib had no choice but to return home in disgrace.

Soon after, Hezekiah became extremely ill. But Isaiah told him he wouldn't die; instead he would live for fifteen more years. Having heard that Hezekiah was sick, the king of Babylon sent messengers who brought greetings and presents to him. Hezekiah welcomed them and showed them his house and all his treasures. But Isaiah warned him that the Lord had said, "These treasures will be carried away to Babylon; nothing will be left and some of your own sons will be servants in the palace of the king of Babylon."

The Babylonian Captivity and Return

Fall of the Kingdom of Judah
(II Kings 21, 25)

The people of Judah did what was evil in God's eyes. After Hezekiah died, his son Manasseh became king. He was very wicked and even sacrificed his own children to idols. So the Lord punished the kingdom of Judah also.

The army of the mighty Nebuchadnezzar, king of Babylon, took Jerusalem, burned the temple and the city, and tore down its walls. Zedekiah, the last king of Judah, was captured and brought before the King of Babylon, who made Zedekiah watch while his own children were killed. Then Zedekiah's eyes were put out. He was put in chains and carried away to Babylon into captivity, together with the people of Judah. [This took place in 587 B.C.]

The Babylonian Captivity
(Daniel 2, 6)

Because the sins of the Israelites were so great, their punishment was heavy. They wanted to return to Jerusalem to worship in the temple of the Lord, but they had to live among heathens in Babylon. Yet the Lord sent them two great prophets, Ezekiel and Daniel, to comfort and strengthen them while they were still in captivity.

One night King Nebuchadnezzar had such a strange dream he could not understand it. So Daniel prayed to the Lord, and that night God revealed both the dream and its meaning in a vision. Then Daniel went to the king and explained that the king had seen a huge statue whose head was gold, whose breast and arms were silver, whose middle and thighs were brass, and whose legs were iron and clay. But a stone, which was not thrown by anyone, struck the image and broke it to pieces; then the stone became a mountain so great that it filled the whole earth.

Daniel went on to interpret the dream for the king. He said that there would be four great kingdoms that would rise up, one after the other, but that the Lord would establish a kingdom that would overthrow all of these and would last forever. The king answered, "Your God is truly God of all gods since he can reveal this mysterious dream."

As a result, Daniel was made chief governor over the wise men of Babylon and was held in high esteem, even after Nebuchadnezzar died. Nonetheless, Daniel did have enemies who had Nebuchadnezzar's successor throw Daniel into a den of lions. But the Lord sent his angel to shut the lions' mouths. On the next day, Daniel was taken up unhurt out of the den, and his enemies who had accused him of wrongdoing were thrown into it instead.

Return From Babylon
(Ezra; Nehemiah)

The first year that Cyrus was king of Persia he conquered Babylon and allowed the Israelites to return to Jerusalem.

The king also restored all the gold and silver vessels that Nebuchadnezzar had taken from the temple. So, just as Jeremiah had prophesied, the seventy years had now gone by and 50,000 Israelites traveled home to Jerusalem, led by Zerubbabel, a chief of the house of David. Two years after their return, they began to build a new temple on Mount Moriah, the site of the former temple which King Solomon had built. There was local opposition to the building of the temple, so construction was delayed for several years. But God sent the prophets Haggai and Zechariah, who encouraged the people to keep building, and the temple was eventually finished.

Some years after this, Ezra, who was from the tribe of Levi, came to Jerusalem from Babylon to teach God's law. He warned the men never again to sin against the Lord by marrying heathen women.

Although the temple was fmished, the walls of Jerusalem had not yet been rebuilt. When Nehemiah, servant to the king of Persia, heard this, he asked the king for permission to go to Judea to rebuild Jerusalem. So the king made him governor of Judea, and he got the walls of Jerusalem built in fifty-two days.

Other Key Sections of the Old Testament

Job
(Job)

Job was the name of a God-fearing, honest man who had seven sons and three daughters. He owned 7,000 sheep, 3,000 camels, 500 yoke of oxen, and 500 female donkeys. He was the wealthiest among all the people of the East. His Sons often feasted together, and when a celebration ended, Job would get up early to offer burnt offerings. He said, "It may be that my sons have sinned and abandoned God in their hearts."

One day, when Job's children were eating and drinking wine at the oldest brother's house, a messenger came to Job and said, "The oxen were plowing and the donkeys were grazing nearby, but the Sabbeans came and took them away, and they have killed the servants. I am the only one who escaped." Before he was done speaking, another messenger came and said, "Fire fell from heaven and burned up the sheep and the shepherds. I am the only one who escaped." While he was still speaking, a third messenger came and said, "The Chaldeans raided the camels and took them, and they killed the servants with swords. I am the only one who escaped." Yet another messenger came and said, "Your sons and daughters were eating and drinking at your eldest son's house. Suddenly, a strong wind came across the desert and blew down the house and killed all of them. I am the only one who escaped."

At this Job tore his clothes and fell to the ground to worship. "I came naked out of my mother's womb," he said, "and naked I shall return. The Lord gave and the Lord has taken away. Blessed be the name of the Lord."

Through all of this Job did not sin or accuse God of any wrongdoing. Job's health failed next, and his body was now covered with boils. He took a piece of pottery to scrape himself, and he sat in ashes.

His wife asked whether he still believed in God, and Job answered, "You speak as a foolish person. Should we receive good at the hand of God but not receive bad also?" Job still did not sin.

Three of Job's friends, hearing of his catastrophe, came to comfort him. But when they saw him, they did not recognize him. They sat with him for seven days, not speaking a word to him, because they saw how much pain he was in. When they did speak, their words were harsh. They thought that Job must be a worse sinner than other people because God punished him so much more than others.

Finally, Job sinned by boasting about his perfection before God and arguing with God. Then the Lord spoke to him out of a whirlwind, saying, "Who is this that dares contend with God?" So Job repented and said, "I have spoken about that which I do not understand." And the Lord forgave Job, but reprimanded his three friends because they had judged Job so severely.

God blessed Job, healed him, and gave him twice as many riches as he had before. Job also had born to him seven more sons and seven more daughters, and he lived to be very old.

Jonah
(Jonah)

The word of the Lord came to the prophet Jonah, saying, "Go immediately to the great city of Ninevah and proclaim its destruction, for there is much wickedness there." But Jonah tried to avoid doing what God asked and, instead, got aboard a ship. However, the Lord sent a storm that was so bad the ship was in danger of being lost. The sailors on the ship said to one another, "Let's cast lots so we can find out who caused this disaster." And the lot fell on Jonah, so they threw him into the sea. When they did, the sea became calm, and the Lord sent a huge fish to swallow Jonah. He was in the belly of the fish for three days, but then the Lord commanded the fish to spew out Jonah, and it threw him out on dry land.

Now the Lord spoke to Jonah a second time. "Go to Ninevah," he said, "and proclaim there what I told you." So Jonah went to the city and cried out, "In forty days Ninevah will be overthrown." The people of Ninevah believed God's word and repented of their sins.

Even the king took off his robe and sat in sackcloth and ashes, which was an ancient sign of repentance. When God saw this, he changed his mind and spared the city.

But that made Jonah angry and he said, "Wasn't this what I said would happen in the first place? That's why I fled to the ship. I know that you are a gracious God who is slow to anger and who withdraws punishment when people repent." And the Lord asked Jonah, "Is it right for you to be so angry?"

So Jonah left the city, but stayed near it to see what would happen. As he sat outside the city, the Lord caused a plant to spring up to shade Jonah from the sun. This made Jonah very happy, but the next morning God sent a worm to attack the plant so that it withered. When the sun finally came up, God made a scorching east wind. As the sun beat upon Jonah's head, he said, "It would be better for me to die than to live." But the Lord said, "You are concerned about a plant for which you did not labor nor make grow. Should I not be concerned about Ninevah, that great city, where there are more than 120,000 people who do not know their right hand from their left?"

Selections from the Psalms
(Psalms)

[Note: The Book of Psalms has rightly been thought of as the hymn book of ancient Israel. Psalms were sung during worship in the temple and are often quoted in the New Testament. Today, people frequently use the Psalms during private devotions. The following Psalms, quoted from the NRSV Bible, are among the most well known.]

"Happy are those who do not follow the advice of the wicked, or take the path that sinners tread, or sit in the seat of scoffers; but their delight is in the law of the LORD, and on his law they meditate day and night." *(Psalm 1:1–2)*

"O LORD, our Sovereign, how majestic is your name in all the earth! You have set your glory above the heavens. Out of the mouths of babes and infants you have founded a bulwark because of your foes, to silence the enemy and the avenger. When I look at your heavens, the work of your fingers, the moon and the stars that you have established; what are human beings that you are mindful of them, mortals that you care for them? Yet you have made them a little lower than God, and crowned them with glory and honor. You have given them dominion over the works of your hands; you have put all things under their feet, all sheep and oxen, and also the beasts of the field, the birds of the air, and the fish of the sea, whatever passes along the paths of the seas. O LORD, our Sovereign, how majestic is your name in all the earth!" *(Psalm 8)*

"How long, O LORD? Will you forget me forever? How long will you hide your face from me? How long must I bear pain in my soul, and have sorrow in my heart all day long? How long shall my enemy be exalted over me? Consider and answer me, O LORD my God! Give light to my eyes, or I will sleep the sleep of death, and my enemy will say, 'I have prevailed'; my foes will rejoice because I am shaken. But I trusted in your steadfast love; my heart shall rejoice in your salvation. I will sing to the LORD, because he has dealt bountifully with me." *(Psalm 13)*

"Fools say in their hearts, 'There is no God.' They are corrupt, they do abominable deeds; there is no one who does good. The LORD looks down from heaven on humankind to see if there are any who are wise, who seek after God. They have all gone astray, they are all alike perverse; there is no one who does good, no, not one." *(Psalm 14:1–3)*

"I love you, O LORD, my strength. The LORD is my rock, my fortress, and my deliverer, my God, my rock in whom I take refuge, my shield, and the horn of my salvation, my stronghold. I call upon the LORD, who is worthy to be praised, so I shall be saved from my enemies." *(Psalm 18:1–3)*

"My God, my God, why have you forsaken me? Why are you so far from helping me, from the words of my groaning? O my God, I cry by day, but you do not answer; and by night, but find no rest. Yet you are holy, enthroned on the praises of Israel." *(Psalm 22.1–3)*

"The LORD is my shepherd, I shall not want. He makes me lie down in green pastures; he leads me beside still waters; he restores my soul. He leads me in right paths for his name's sake. Even though I walk through the darkest valley, I fear no evil; for you are with me; your rod and your staff—they comfort me. You prepare a table before me in the presence of my enemies; you anoint my head with oil; my cup overflows. Surely goodness and mercy shall follow me all the days of my life, and I shall dwell in the house of the LORD my whole life long." *(Psalm 23)*

"Make me to know your ways, O LORD; teach me your paths. Lead me in your truth, and teach me, for you are the God of my salvation; for you I wait all day long. Be mindful of your mercy, O LORD, and of your steadfast love, for they have been from of old. Do not remember the sins of my youth or my transgressions; according to your steadfast love remember me, for your goodness' sake, O LORD! Good and upright is the LORD; therefore he instructs sinners in the way. He leads the humble in what is right, and teaches the humble his way. All the paths of the LORD are steadfast love and faithfulness, for those who keep his covenant and his decrees." *(Psalm 25:4–10)*

"God is our refuge and strength, a very present help in trouble. Therefore we will not fear, though the earth should change, though the mountains shake in the heart of the sea; though its waters roar and foam, though the mountains tremble with its tumult. There is a river whose streams make glad the city of God, the holy habitation of the Most High. God is in the midst of the city; it shall not be moved; God will help it when the morning dawns. The nations are in an uproar, the kingdoms totter; he utters his voice, the earth melts. The LORD of hosts is with us; the God of Jacob is our refuge. Come, behold the works of the LORD; see what desolations he has brought on the earth. He makes wars cease to the end of the earth; he breaks the bow, and shatters the spear; he burns the shields with fire. 'Be still, and know that I am God! I am exalted among the nations, I am exalted in the earth.' The LORD of hosts is with us; the God of Jacob is our refuge." *(Psalm 46)*

"Have mercy on me, O God, according to your steadfast love; according to your abundant mercy blot out my transgressions. Wash me thoroughly from my iniquity, and cleanse me from my sin. Let me hear joy and gladness; let the bones that you have crushed rejoice. Hide your face from my sins, and blot out all my iniquities. Create in me a clean heart, O God, and put a new and right spirit within me. Do not cast me away from your presence, and do not take your holy spirit from me. Restore to me the joy of your salvation, and sustain in me a willing spirit." *(Psalm 51.1–2, 8–12)*

"But truly God has listened; he has given heed to the words of my prayer. Blessed be God, because he has not rejected my prayer or removed his steadfast love from me." *(Psalm 66:19–20)*

"There is none like you among the gods, O Lord, nor are there any works like yours. All the nations you have made shall come and bow down before you, O Lord, and shall glorify your name. For you are great and do wondrous things; you alone are God. Teach me your way, O LORD, that I may walk in your truth; give me an undivided heart to revere your name. I give thanks to you, O Lord my God, with my whole heart, and I will glorify your name forever." *(Psalm 86.8–12)*

"Praise the LORD! Praise, O servants of the LORD; praise the name of the LORD. Blessed be the name of the LORD from this time on and forevermore. From the rising of the sun to its setting the name of the LORD is to be praised. The LORD is high above all nations, and his glory above the heavens. Who is like the LORD our God, who is seated on high, who looks far down on the heavens and the earth? He raises the poor from the dust, and lifts the needy from the ash heap, to make them sit with princes, with the princes of his people. He gives the barren woman a home, making her the joyous mother of children. Praise the LORD!" *(Psalm 113)*

"I lift up my eyes to the hills—from where will my help come? My help comes from the LORD, who made heaven and earth. He will not let your foot be moved; he who keeps you will not slumber. He who keeps Israel will neither slumber nor sleep. The LORD is your keeper; the LORD is your shade at your right hand. The sun shall not strike you by day, nor the moon by night. The LORD will keep you from all evil; he will keep your life. The LORD will keep your going out and your coming in from this time on and forevermore." *(Psalm 121)*

Books of the Old Testament

Genesis
Exodus
Leviticus
Numbers
Deuteronomy
Joshua
Judges
Ruth
I Samuel
II Samuel
I Kings
II Kings
I Chronicles
II Chronicles
Ezra
Nehemiah
Esther
Job
Psalms
Proverbs

Ecclesiastes
Song of Solomon
Isaiah
Jeremiah
Lamentations
Ezekiel
Daniel
Hosea
Joel
Amos
Obadiah
Jonah
Micah
Nahum
Habakkuk
Zephaniah
Haggai
Zechariah
Malachi

Old Testament Timeline

[Note: All dates provided below are speculative; however, the specific dates in parentheses are based on more convincing historical evidence.]

B.C.

2000
1800   Abraham & Sarah
1700   Isaac & Rebekah
1600   Jacob & Rachel
       Joseph
1500
1400
1300   Moses & the Exodus (early 13th century)
1250   Joshua and the conquest of Canaan (1200, initial occupation)
1200   Judges
1150   The Judges Deborah & Gideon
1100
1050   King Saul (1033 to 1011)
1000   King David (1003 to 971 or 970)
950   King Solomon (971 or 970 to 931 or 930)
       Israel splits into two kingdoms: Israel & Judah (922)
       King Rehoboam of Judah (931 or 930 to 913)
900
850   Elijah
       Elisha
800
750   Fall of Samaria, Kingdom of Israel (722 to 720)
700   King Hezekiah of Judah (716 or 715 to 687 or 676)
       Prophet Micah (742 to 698)
       Prophet Isaiah
650   King Josiah of Judah (641 or 640 to 609)
       Prophet Zephaniah (639 to 609)
       Prophet Nahum (612)
       Reform under King Josiah of Judah (622 or 621)

	Prophet Jeremiah (626 to 587)
600	Prophet Habbakuk (609 to 598)
	Fall of Jerusalem (Kingdom of Judah) & exile to Babylon (587)
550	Exiles return from Babylon (538)
500	Persian Rule (538 to 432)
	Prophet Malachi (486 to 464)
	Ezra (458)
450	Nehemiah (445)
400	
350	Alexander the Great conquest Palestine (334 to 332)
300	
200	
150	Maccabean Revolt (168 to 142)

Between the Testaments

As can be seen from the list on page 44, The Old Testament is not one book, but a set of books. The word for an authoritative list of such books is *canon*. No canon has been firmly established for the Old Testament, which was compiled in both Hebrew and Greek. Protestants have recognized as canonical only those books which appeared in the Hebrew version of the Old Testament. In contrast, the Eastern Orthodox Church and, to a lesser extent, the Roman Catholic Church have recognized only those in the Greek version. Protestants refer to the books in the Greek version as the *Apocrypha*. For Protestants, *apocrypha* is a word which means 'hidden.' The following books constitute the Apocrypha and are usually listed between the Old and New Testaments. The type of literature in these books is varied, as it is in the entire Old Testament.

Canonical for Eastern Orthodox Church and Roman Catholic Church:
Tobit
Judith
The Additions to the Book of Esther
The Wisdom of Solomon
Ecclesiasticus
Baruch
The Letter of Jeremiah
The Prayer of Azariah and the Son of the Three Jews
Susanna
Bel and the Dragon
I & II Maccabees

Canonical for Eastern Orthodox Church but not Roman Catholic Church:
The Prayer of Manasseh
I Esdras
III Maccabees
Psalm 151
IV Maccabees (stands in an appendix in Eastern Orthodox Bibles)

[Note: In the New Testament, all 27 books are recognized as canonical by Eastern Orthodox, Roman Catholic, and Protestant Christians.]

THE NEW TESTAMENT

The Gospels
(Matthew, Mark, Luke, and John)

Birth of John the Baptist and Jesus

Birth of John the Baptist
(Luke 1:5–25, 57–66, 80)

When Herod the Great was king of Judea, there was a priest named Zechariah who had a wife named Elizabeth. They were both devout people, but they had no children and were getting old. One day when Zechariah was making an offering in the temple and the people were praying outside, an angel of the Lord appeared to him. Zechariah was afraid, but the angel said, "Fear not, Zechariah, because your prayer has been heard. Your wife will have a son, and you will name him John. He will go out in the spirit and power of Elijah, and prepare the people for the Lord."

Zechariah said, "How will I know if what you say is true?" And the angel said, "I am Gabriel, and I stand in the presence of God. I was sent to tell you the truth, but because you did not believe, you will lose your ability to speak until the day that these things happen." And so it happened that Elizabeth gave birth to a son. Her neighbors and relatives thought that the child should be named Zechariah after his father. But Elizabeth said, "He will be named John." They said, "None of your relatives is named John," and they made signs to Zechariah to find out what he thought the boy should be named. He asked for something to write on and wrote, "His name is John." Immediately, Zechariah's mouth was opened and he spoke, praising God. The child grew up and became strong spiritually. He stayed in the wilderness until the day when he appeared before the people in Israel.

Announcement to Mary
(Luke 1:26–38)

Six months after Gabriel had appeared to Zechariah, God sent the same angel to Nazareth, a city of Galilee. There the angel appeared to a virgin, whose name was Mary and who was engaged to Joseph. The angel said to her, "Greetings, Mary. You are favored by God! The Lord is with you." But she was troubled at what she heard and wondered what it all meant. But the angel said, "Don't be afraid, Mary. You will bear a son, and he will be named Jesus [which means 'Savior']." Then Mary said, "How can this be? I am a virgin." The angel answered, "The Holy Spirit will be with you. Therefore, the child that is born will be holy and will be called the Son of God." So Mary said, "I am the Lord's servant; let it happen just as you have said." And the angel went away.

Birth of Jesus
(Matthew 1:18–2:23, Luke 2:1–20)

During those days, the Emperor Caesar Augustus ordered that all the world should be taxed. In order to do that, all the people were to be registered in their home towns. So Joseph and Mary traveled from Nazareth in Galilee to the city of David (which is called Bethlehem) in Judea to be registered. Mary was expecting a child, and while they were there, the time came for her to deliver the baby. She gave birth to a son, wrapped him in pieces of cloth, and laid him down in a manger because the inn was full.

In that same country there were shepherds in the fields watching over their flocks at night. The angel of the Lord came to them, and a bright light was shining all around them, so they were afraid. But the angel said to them, "Don't be afraid. I am bringing good news that will give you great joy. Today, in the city of David, a Savior was born who is Christ the Lord. Look for this sign—you will find a baby wrapped in pieces of cloth, lying in a manger." Suddenly this angel was joined by a multitude of angels praising God and saying, "Glory to God in the highest and peace among all those he favors on earth."

Wise Men From the East
(Matthew 2:1–23)

When Jesus was born in Bethlehem (at the time when Herod the Great was king), wise men came to Jerusalem asking, "Where is the one who was born the King of the Jews? We saw his star from the East and have come to worship him." Herod, hearing this, called the chief priests and scribes together and asked them where the Christ was to be born. They answered, "In Bethlehem, as it was foretold by Micah the prophet." Then Herod secretly called the wise men and asked them exactly the time when the star they had seen appeared. Then he said to them, "Go to Bethlehem and search diligently for the child. When you find him, bring me word so I can come and worship him too.

The wise men then departed, following the star, and it led them to the place where the child was. When they saw him with his mother, they fell to their knees and worshiped him. Then they opened their treasures and gave the child gold, frankincense, and myrrh. And because God warned them in a dream that they should not return to Herod, they went back to their own country by another route.

When they left, the angel of the Lord appeared to Joseph in a dream and said, "Arise! Take the child and his mother and go to Egypt because Herod is looking for the child and wants to kill him. Stay there until I tell you that you can return." So that night Joseph took the child and his mother Mary and went to Egypt.

When Herod realized that the wise men had tricked him by not returning, he was furious and so he killed all the male children in Bethlehem who were two years old and under. When Herod the Great died, an angel said to Joseph, "Arise. Take the child and Mary and go to Israel because those who sought to kill the child are dead."

So they went to the town of Nazareth in Galilee and made their home there.

Boy Jesus in the Temple
(Luke 2:4 –52)

Jesus' parents went to Jerusalem every year for the Passover feast; and when Jesus was twelve years old, they took him with them. After the Passover, Joseph and Mary started home for Nazareth, but Jesus stayed in Jerusalem. His parents thought that he was somewhere in their group of travelers, so they traveled a full day's journey toward home before discovering that Jesus wasn't with them. They immediately returned to Jerusalem to search for him. Three days later they found him in the temple, sitting with the teachers, listening to them and asking questions. Everyone who heard Jesus was astonished at his understanding and answers. But his mother said, "Son, why did you do this to us? Your father and I have been searching everywhere for you." Jesus answered, "Why were you looking for me? Didn't you know that I would be in my father's house?" His parents didn't understand his answer, but he obeyed them and went with them back to Nazareth. As Jesus grew older, his wisdom increased as did his stature in the eyes of God and the people.

Jesus' Ministry

John the Baptist and the Baptism of Jesus (Matthew 3:1–17; Mark 1:1–11; Luke 3:1–22; John 1:6–8, 19–34)

Just as the prophets had told the people of Israel, John the Baptist was in the wilderness doing the work they described: "See, I [God] am sending a messenger ahead of you, who will prepare your way by crying out in the wilderness: 'Prepare the way of the Lord.'" John the Baptist was this messenger and he preached about a baptism of repentance for the forgiveness of sins. He wore clothes made out of camel's hair and a leather belt around his waist, and he ate locusts and wild honey.

People from Jerusalem and the surrounding country went to hear what John said. He baptized them in the Jordan River and they confessed their sins. But he said to them, "The one who is more powerful than I am [Jesus] is coming after me; I am not even worthy to untie his sandals. I baptize you with water but he will baptize you with the Holy Spirit."

Jesus did come from Nazareth in Galilee and was also baptized by John in the Jordan River. When Jesus came out of the water, he saw the heavens open, and the Spirit of God descended on him like a dove. And a voice from heaven said, "You are my beloved Son; with you I am well pleased."

Jesus is Tempted by the Devil
(Matthew 4:1–11; Mark 1:12–13; Luke 4:1–13)

Jesus was led by the Spirit into the wilderness, where he fasted for forty days and forty nights, becoming extremely hungry. Then the devil came to him and said, "If you are the Son of God, command these stones to become bread." Jesus answered, "Human beings do not live by bread alone, but by every word that comes from God's mouth." Next the devil took Jesus to Jerusalem, set him on the pinnacle of the temple, and said, "If you are the Son of God, throw yourself down. It is written that God will command his angels to care for you so that you do not even hit your foot against a stone." But Jesus answered, "Again it is written, do not tempt the Lord your God."

Then, the devil took Jesus to a very high mountain and showed him all the kingdoms of the earth and their glory. He said, "I will give you all these things if you will fall down and worship me." Jesus said to him, "Go away, Satan! It is written, 'worship the Lord your God and him only should you serve." Then the devil left and angels immediately came and cared for Jesus.

Jesus Chooses His Disciples
(Matthew 4:18–22, 10:1–4; Mark 1:16–20, 3:13–19,
Luke 5:1–11, 6:12–16; John 1:35–51)

As Jesus walked on the shore of the Sea of Galilee, he saw two brothers, Andrew and Simon, the latter of whom was called Peter. They were fishermen who were busy casting their nets into the water. Jesus said to them, "Follow me, and you will fish for people." They left their nets at once and followed him. As Jesus continued on his way, he saw two sons of Zebedee, James and John, mending their fishing nets. Jesus called to them and they, too, immediately left their father and followed Jesus.

[Note: Eventually, Jesus chose twelve disciples. In addition to Peter, Andrew, James, and John, he chose Philip, Bartholomew, Thomas, Matthew, James (son of Alphaeus), Thaddaeus, Simon (the Cananaean), and Judas Iscariot.]

Turning Water into Wine
(John 2:1–11)

One day there was a wedding in Cana, a town in Galilee; and Jesus, his mother, and his disciples were invited. When the wine ran out, Jesus' mother said to him, "They don't have any more wine." He answered, "How is that my concern? The time to reveal my glory has not yet come." She said to the servants, "Do whatever he asks you to do."

Now the Jews always washed their hands before eating as a ritual of purification, so there were six large jars there for that purpose. Jesus told the servants, "Fill those jars to the top with water." After they did, he said, "Draw some out and bring it to the host." When the host had tasted what was in the cup [without knowing where it came from], he said to the bridegroom, "Everyone else serves the good wine first, but you have saved the good wine for now. ' By turning the water into wine, his first miracle, Jesus revealed his glory and his disciples believed in him.

Nicodemus
(John 3:1–21)

Nicodemus, a Pharisee and a leader among the religious authorities, came to Jesus one night and said to him, "Rabbi, we know you're a teacher who has come from God because no one could perform the miracles you have without God." Jesus replied, "No one will see the kingdom of God without being born from above." Nicodemus said, "How can someone be born after growing old? Can a person again enter a mother's womb and be born a second time?" Jesus answered, "What I tell you is true. No one can enter God's kingdom without being born of water and the Spirit. What is born of the flesh is flesh, and what is born of the Spirit is spirit. Don't be surprised by what I say." Nicodemus asked, "How can this be?"

Jesus replied, "You are a teacher of Israel and don't know these things? If I tell you about earthly things and you do not believe, how can you believe if I tell you about heavenly things? No one has gone up into heaven except the one who came down from heaven, the Son of Man [Jesus was referring to himself]. Just as Moses lifted up the serpent in the wilderness, so must the Son of Man be lifted [on the cross], so that all who believe in him will have eternal life. For God so loved the world that he gave his only Son, so that no one who believes in him will perish, but instead will have eternal life."

Woman of Samaria
(John 4:4–42)

Jesus was traveling through Samaria and, being tired from the journey, he sat down by Jacob's Well, which was near the city of Sychar. As he rested, a Samaritan woman came to get some water from the well, and Jesus said to her, "Give me a drink." [At that time Jews and Samaritans had no dealings with each other.] So she asked, "How can you, a Jew, ask for a drink of water from me, a Samaritan?" Jesus said, "If you knew who I am, you would have asked me and I would have given you living water." She said to him, "But you don't have anything with which to draw water from this deep well." Jesus answered her, "Go and get your husband and then come back here." She replied, "I don't have a husband." Jesus said, "You told the truth when you said that you don't have a husband. In fact, you have had five husbands, and the man with whom you are currently living is not your husband."

The woman said to him, "I see that you are a prophet. We Samaritans believe that people ought to worship God on this mountain, but the Jews say that people should worship in Jerusalem." Jesus said, "The time is coming when true worshipers will not be concerned about where they worship but, instead, with how they worship: in spirit and truth." The woman said, "When the Messiah comes, he will preach the truth to us." Jesus said to her, "I am the Messiah." When she heard this, the woman left in such a hurry that she left her water jar behind, and she went into the city and told everyone what had happened to her. And many Samaritans from Sychar then believed in Jesus because the woman said, "He was able to tell me everything I have ever done." Many of them went out to the well to see Jesus. Later the people said, "It's no longer because of the woman's testimony that we believe; now we've heard for ourselves. This is truly the Savior of the world."

The Sermon on the Mount
(Matthew 5–7)

Once Jesus addressed the people from atop a mountain, [so this was called the Sermon on the Mount]. His disciples joined him, and he began to teach everyone gathered. [The first teachings in this sermon, Matthew 5:3–12, have become known as the Beatitudes and are quoted from the NRSV Bible.]

> "Blessed are the poor in spirit, for theirs is the kingdom of heaven."
>
> "Blessed are those who mourn, for they will be comforted."
>
> "Blessed are the meek, for they will inherit the earth."
>
> "Blessed are those who hunger and thirst for righteousness, for they will be filled."
>
> "Blessed are the merciful, for they will receive mercy."
>
> "Blessed are the pure in heart, for they will see God."
>
> "Blessed are the peacemakers, for they will be called children of God."
>
> "Blessed are those who are persecuted for righteousness' sake, for theirs is the kingdom of heaven."
>
> "Blessed are you when people revile you and persecute you and utter all kinds of evil against you falsely on my account. Rejoice and be glad, for your reward is great in heaven, for in the same way they persecuted the prophets who were before you."

[These other teachings in this sermon are also quoted from the NRSV Bible.]

> "I did not come to destroy the law and the prophets, but to fulfill them."
>
> "You heard it said, 'You shall not murder.' But I say that if you are even angry with a brother or sister, you will be judged."
>
> "You heard it said, 'You shall not commit adultery.' But I say that everyone who even looks at a woman with lust has already committed adultery with her in his heart."

"When you pray, do not act like the hypocrites. They love to pray while standing in the synagogues and on street corners so that everyone can see them. But when you pray, go into your room and shut the door. Pray to the Father in secret and your Father will reward you."

[Note: At this point in the Sermon on the Mount, Jesus taught the people the Lord's Prayer. See Matthew 6:9–13 and Luke 11:2–4. The text of the Lord's Prayer is also in the Appendix of this book.]

"Do not collect material possessions for yourselves. Rather, build up treasures in heaven. Where your treasure is, your heart will be also."

"Do not worry about what you will eat, what you will drink, or what you will wear. Look at the birds. They neither plant nor harvest, yet your heavenly Father feeds them. Aren't you worth more than they are? Consider the lilies of the field and how they grow. They don't work to make their own clothes, yet even King Solomon in all his glory was not dressed as beautifully. Therefore, don't worry about tomorrow. Today's troubles are enough for today."

"Always do to others what you would want them to do to you."

Raising a Widow's Son From the Dead
(Luke 7:11–17)

As Jesus approached a town called Nain, there was a dead man being carried out of town to be buried. He was the only son of a widow, and a large crowd followed her to the burial. When Jesus saw her, he had compassion for her and said, "Don't weep." And he came and touched the coffin, saying, "Young man, I say to you, rise." At that moment, the dead man sat up and began to speak. The people in the crowd were afraid, and they glorified God saying, "A great prophet is among us. God has visited his people."

Parable of the Sower and its Interpretation
(Matthew 13:3–8, 18–23; Mark 4:1–9, 13–20; Luke 8:4–8, 11–15)

Jesus said, "A farmer went out to plant; and as he sowed, some seeds fell on the path, and birds ate them. Other seeds fell on rocky places, and they sprang up quickly because the soil was not deep. But when the sun came up, they got scorched; and since they had no roots, they withered. And still other seeds fell where there were thorns; when the thorns grew, they choked the seeds and killed them. But some seeds fell in good soil and produced abundant fruit."

The disciples asked about the parable and Jesus said, "Don't you understand? The sower sows the word of God. What falls on the path is like people who hear the word, but when they do, Satan comes and takes it away. That which falls on rocky places is like people who hear the word and immediately receive it with joy, but when trouble comes their way, they turn away from God because they have no root. What lands among the thorns is like those who hear the word, but allow concerns of this world and the lure of wealth to choke out the word so that it bears no fruit. But that which is sown into good soil is like those who hear the word and keep it in their hearts so that it bears abundant fruit."

Parable of the Weeds Among the Wheat and its Interpretation
(Matthew 13:24–30, 36–43)

Jesus said that the kingdom of heaven is like a man who planted wheat seeds in his field; but during the night, the man's enemy came and sowed weeds among the good seeds. So when the plants sprang up, weeds also appeared. The farmer's servants came and said to him, "Sir, didn't you plant good seeds in your field? Why are there weeds?" He answered, "An enemy did this to me." The servants said, "Do you want us to pick the weeds?" He answered, "No, I don't want to uproot the wheat along with the weeds. Let both grow together until the harvest. Then I'll tell the reapers to gather the weeds first, bind them in bundles, and burn them. Then they can gather the wheat into my barn."

The disciples asked Jesus to explain this parable, so he told them this: "The one who sows the good seeds is the Son of Man, the field is the world, and the good seeds are the children of the kingdom. The enemy who sowed the weeds is the devil, and the weeds are his children. The harvest is the end of the world. At that time, the Son of Man will send his angels, and they will gather all those who do evil and cast them into hell. Then the righteous will shine like the sun in their Father's kingdom."

Stilling a Storm
(Matthew 8:23–27; Mark 4:36–41; Luke 8:22–24)

Jesus and his disciples were in a boat on the Sea of Galilee one evening when a violent storm came up. The wind blew so hard that the boat began to take on water. But Jesus was in the back of the boat, asleep. His disciples woke him up, saying, "Teacher, don't you care that we are about to die?!" Jesus got up and spoke sharply to the wind and the waves, saying, "Peace! Be still! ," and there was total calm. The he said to them, "Why are you afraid? Do you have so little faith?" The disciples were amazed and said, "Who is this that even the wind and the sea obey him?"

Raising Jairus' Daughter From the Dead
(Matthew 9:18–26; Mark 5:21–43; Luke 8:40–56)

Jairus, who was the ruler of a synagogue, came and fell at Jesus' feet saying, "My little daughter is near death. Please, come and save her." Jesus went with him, but on the way they met some people from Jairus' house who said, "Your daughter has died." Jesus said to the father, "Don't be afraid, but believe." When Jesus entered the house, everyone was crying. Jesus said, "Why are you crying? The girl is not dead, but sleeping." They laughed at him, but he sent them all outside and took Jairus and his wife, along with Peter, James, and John, and went in to the child. Jesus said, "Little girl, I say to you, arise." And she got up and walked around.

Death of John the Baptist
(Matthew 14:1–12; Mark 6:14–29; Luke 9:7–9)

John continued to call all people to repentance, even King Herod Antipas (son of Herod the Great). This king forced his brother to divorce his wife, Herodias, so that the king could marry her himself. But John the Baptist said to the king, "It is not right for you to take her for your wife." Herodias was offended, so she had King Herod's men arrest John and put him in prison. On the king's birthday, the daughter of Herodias danced for him and the guests. Herod was so pleased that he promised to give the girl whatever she asked for, even if it was half of his kingdom. She left and consulted her mother, who, still angry with John, said, "Ask for the head of John the Baptist on a platter." When the king heard the request he was deeply disturbed, but to keep the promise he had made in front of his guests, he did as she asked. So John was beheaded, and his head was brought to the princess and her mother on a platter. When John's followers heard what had happened, they went and got his body and buried him.

Feeding the Five Thousand
(Matthew 14:13–21; Mark 6:30–44; Luke 9:10–17; John 6:1–13)

Seeking some rest, Jesus and his disciples went by boat on the Sea of Galilee to a deserted location, but the people saw them and followed on foot along the shore, arriving before the boat. When evening fell, the disciples said to Jesus, "There is nothing here for the people to eat. Send them away into the surrounding villages so they can buy themselves some food." Jesus said, "You give them something to eat." They said, "We only have five loaves of bread and two fish. How can we feed so many with so little?"

Jesus told them to tell everyone to sit down on the grass. Then he took the five loaves and two fish, looked up to heaven, blessed the food, and gave it to the disciples, who passed it out to the people. After everyone had eaten as much as they wanted, Jesus said to the disciples, "Put what is left in baskets so that nothing is wasted," and they filled twelve baskets of food. Five thousand men ate that evening in addition to women and children.

A Syrophoenician Woman's Faith
(Matthew 15:21–28; Mark 7:24–30)

When Jesus was traveling in the region of Tyre, he went into a house because he did not want anyone to know he was in the area. But a Syrophoenician woman, a Gentile, heard he was there and found him. She begged him to have mercy on her daughter who was possessed by a demon. Jesus answered, "Let the children [of Israel, the Jews] be fed first. It's not fair to take food for children and give it to dogs." She replied, "Yes, Lord, but even dogs get to eat the crumbs that fall under the children's table." And Jesus said, "Woman, your words show that you have great faith. Your daughter is healed." So the woman went home and found her child no longer possessed by the demon.

The Transfiguration
(Matthew 17:1–9; Mark 9:2–10; Luke 9:28–36)

One day, Jesus took Peter, James, and John up to a high mountain. Jesus' appearance changed [transfigured] before their eyes. His face was shining like the sun and his clothes became dazzling white. Suddenly, Moses and Elijah appeared to them and spoke with Jesus. Peter said to Jesus, "Teacher, it is good for us to be here. Let's make three houses, one for you, one for Moses, and one for Elijah." (Peter did not know what to say because he and the other disciples were terrified.) Then a cloud overshadowed them and a voice coming from the cloud said, "This is my beloved Son. Listen to him." Suddenly, they looked around and saw no one with them but Jesus. As they went down the mountain Jesus said, "Don't tell anyone about what you've seen here until the Son of Man has been raised from the dead." So they said nothing about what happened but wondered what being "raised from the dead" could mean.

Parable of the Unforgiving Servant
(Matthew 18:21–35)

Peter came to Jesus and asked, "If someone sins against me, how often should I forgive this person? Seven times?" Jesus answered, "Not seven times, but seventy times seven." And he told this parable:

"The Kingdom of God can be compared to a king who wanted to settle accounts with his servants who owed him money. First, a servant who owed him ten thousand talents [a large sum] was brought to him. He was not able to pay, so the king ordered him to be sold, together with his wife and children. But the servant fell to his knees and said, 'Master, be patient with me, and I will repay you everything.' The king pitied him, so the servant was released and his debt was forgiven."

"But that same servant went out and found one of his fellow servants who owed him a small sum of money. He grabbed him by the throat and said, 'Pay me what you owe.' His fellow servant fell down on his knees saying, 'Be patient with me. I will pay you everything.' But the first servant refused and had the other man put in prison."

"When the other servants saw what had happened, they were upset and told the king what they had seen. So the king called for the unforgiving servant and said, 'You wicked servant. I forgave your entire debt because you begged me. Shouldn't you, then, have had compassion for your fellow servant as I had compassion for you?' In anger, the king cast him into prison until he could pay the whole debt. My heavenly Father will do the same to you if you do not sincerely forgive those who sin against you."

Parable of the Good Samaritan
(Luke 10:25–37)

Once a lawyer tried to test Jesus. He said, "Teacher, what must I do to receive eternal life?" Jesus said to him, "What does the law say?" The lawyer answered, "You must love the Lord your God with all your heart, soul, strength, and mind, and you must love your neighbor as yourself." And Jesus said, "You gave the right answer. Do that and you will live." But the lawyer wanted to justify himself, so he asked, "Who is my neighbor?"

Jesus answered him by saying, "A man who was going from Jerusalem to Jericho was attacked by robbers. They stripped him, beat him, and left him for dead. By chance, a priest was going down that road and, seeing the beaten man, passed by on the other side of the road. A Levite did the same thing. But a Samaritan [an enemy of the injured man's people] came near the man and, when he saw him, had compassion on him. The Samaritan went to him, bandaged his wounds, and set the man on his donkey to bring him to an inn where he could receive care. The next day the Samaritan had to leave, but he gave money to the innkeeper and said, 'Take care of him and if you spend more than this, I will repay you when I come back.' Which of these three," asked Jesus, "do you think, was a neighbor to the man who was beaten by robbers?" The lawyer answered, "The one who showed him mercy." And Jesus said, "Go and do the same."

Parable of the Rich Fool
(Luke 12:16–21)

Jesus said, "A rich man's land produced a plentiful harvest and he thought to himself, 'What can I do? I don't have enough room to store my crop.' And he said, 'I know what to do. I'll tear down my barns and build bigger ones, so I can store all of my crop. Then I can take time to eat, drink, and be merry.' But God said to him, 'You fool. Tonight your life will be taken from you; you are going to die. Then who will own those riches which you have stored up?" Jesus said, "It is the same for all those who collect material things for themselves but are not rich in their relationship with God."

Parable of the Fig Tree
(Luke 13:6–9)

Jesus said, "A man had planted a fig tree in his vineyard, but when he went to look for fruit on it, there was none. So he said to his gardener, 'I have been looking for fruit on this fig tree for three years and still have none. Cut it down. Why should it take up space?' But the gardener said, 'Keep it one more year. I'll dig around it and fertilize it; maybe it will bear fruit next year. If not, then you can cut it down."

[Note: The threat of the fig tree's destruction is a metaphor for God's judgment. What is significant in this parable is that even as a judgment is pronounced, a reprieve is granted. More time is allowed for one to "bear the fruit" of repentance. That judgment is only delayed, however, as the tree was given just one more year to bear fruit.]

Parable of the Lost Sheep
(Luke 15:3–7)

Jesus said, "If you had 100 sheep and lost one, wouldn't you leave the 99 and go look for the lost one until you found it? And when you found it, wouldn't you carry it back on your shoulders and rejoice more over that one sheep than over the 99 which were never lost? In the same way, there will be more rejoicing in heaven over one repentant sinner than over 99 who are righteous and seek no repentance."

Parable of the Two Sons [or the Prodigal Son]
(Luke 15:11–32)

Jesus said, "A certain man had two sons. The younger one said to his father, 'Give me my share of the inheritance.' So the father divided his goods between the sons. Then the younger son took all that was his and went to a country far away, where he wasted his inheritance in reckless living. When he had spent it all, a disastrous famine hit the country."

"As a result, he needed money, so he became the servant of a man in that country and was sent into the fields to feed hogs. He would have gladly eaten what he gave the pigs, but no one gave him anything. When he came to his senses he said to himself, 'How many of my father's hired servants have enough bread to eat and even have some to spare? And here I am dying of hunger!' So he decided to go home and say to his father, 'I have committed sins against heaven and against you and am no longer worthy to be called your son. Make me one of your servants.' So he set off for his father's home. But when he was still a long way off, his father saw him and ran to hug and kiss him. And the son said to him, 'Father, I have committed sins against heaven and against you and am no longer worthy to be called your son.' But the father said to his servants, 'Bring out the best robe and put it on him. And put a ring on his finger and shoes on his feet. Kill the fatted calf so we can eat and celebrate. My son who was dead is alive again: he was lost and now he is found!"

"Now the older son had been working in the field, and when he came home, he heard music and dancing. He asked the servants what was going on, and hearing that his father was having a celebration for his brother who had returned, he was angry and would not go in. His father came out and pleaded with him to join them. But the older son said, 'For many years I worked like a slave for you and never disobeyed you, yet you have never given me so much as a goat, much less a fatted calf, to eat with my friends. But as soon as this son of yours comes home after throwing away all his money on prostitutes, you killed the fatted calf for him!' But his father said, 'Son, you have always been with me and all that I have is yours. But it was the right thing to do to celebrate because it was as if your brother was dead and is alive again. He was lost and has now been found."

Parable of the Rich Man and Lazarus
(Luke 16:19–31)

Jesus said, "There was a rich man who wore fine linen and ate sumptuous food every day. But at the gate of his house lay a beggar named Lazarus, who was full of sores and wanted only to be fed the crumbs that fell from the rich man's table. Even dogs came and licked his sores."

"When the beggar died, angels brought him to be with Abraham in heaven. The rich man also died, but he was sent to hell, where he was tormented. From there, he saw Abraham far off in heaven, with Lazarus by his side. And he cried out saying, 'Abraham, have mercy on me and send Lazarus to put his fingers in water and then cool my tongue; I am being tormented by these flames.' But Abraham said, 'Remember that all your life you received only good things. In contrast, Lazarus received only inferior things. Now he is comforted and you are in agony. Besides, there is a great chasm between us and you, which no one can cross."

"So the man said, 'I beg you, Abraham, please send Lazarus to my father's house to talk to my five brothers. Let him warn them so that they will not end up in this place of torment.' Abraham answered, 'They already have Moses and the prophets to warn them.' But the man said, 'No, Abraham. Only if someone comes back from the dead will they repent.' Abraham replied, 'If they won't listen to Moses and the prophets, they won't be persuaded by someone who comes back from the dead either.'"

Healing Ten Lepers
(Luke 17:11–19)

On his way to Jerusalem, Jesus met ten lepers. Keeping their distance from him, they cried out, "Jesus, Master, have mercy on us." He said to them, "Go and show the priests your condition." As they went to do so, they were cured. One of them, a Samaritan, after seeing that he was healed, went back to find Jesus. With a loud voice, he shouted praises to God and fell down at Jesus' feet, giving him thanks. Then Jesus said, "Weren't ten healed? Where are the other nine? Wasn't anyone interested in giving glory to God except this stranger?" He said to him, "Get up; your faith is what made you well."

Parable of the Pharisee and the Tax Collector
(Luke 18:9–14)

There were some who believed in their own goodness but hated others, so Jesus told them this parable: "Two men, one a Pharisee and the other a tax collector, went to the temple to pray. The Pharisee stood and prayed, 'God, I thank you that I am not like other men: thieves, adulterers, or even this tax collector. I fast twice a week. I give away 10% of all that I earn.' But the tax collector, who stood far away, would not even look up toward heaven. He beat his chest, saying, 'God have mercy on me, a sinner!' I'm telling you that this tax collector went home justified, but not the Pharisee. Those who exalt themselves will be humbled, but those who humble themselves will be exalted."

Blessing the Children
(Matthew 19:13–15; Mark 10:13–16; Luke 18:15–17)

People often brought little children to Jesus so that he would put his hands on them and bless them, even though the disciples sternly told the people not to let their children get near Jesus. But Jesus said, "Let the children come to me; don't stop them. The kingdom of God belongs to little ones like these. I tell you, truly, that whoever doesn't see the kingdom of God as a little child does will never enter it." And Jesus took the children in his arms and blessed them.

Parable of the Laborers in the Vineyard
(Matthew 20:1–16)

Jesus said, "The kingdom of heaven is like a farmer who went out early in the morning to hire laborers to work in his vineyard. After agreeing on their pay, he sent them to work. Later that morning, he went out and saw others standing idle in the market place, so he said to them, 'Go work in my vineyard and I'll pay you whatever is right.' Around noon and again later that afternoon he went out and did the same thing. At those times, he found others still standing idle, so he said to them, 'Why are you standing here idle all day?' They answered, 'Because no one hired us.' He said, 'Go work in my vineyard and I'll pay you whatever is right.'"

"At the end of the day, the owner of the vineyard said to his manager, 'Call all the workers and give them their pay, beginning with those who were hired last.' So those hired late in the day came and received a full day's wage. When those hired first came for their pay, they assumed they would be paid more than the others, but they also received one day's wage. This made them angry, and they said to the farmer, 'These people worked only one hour, but you paid them the same amount of money as you paid us who endured the heat of the entire day.' But the farmer answered, 'I did nothing wrong. Didn't you agree to work for one day's wage? Take the pay that belongs to you and go. I choose to pay the last hired the same as I pay the first hired. Is it against the law for me to do what I want with my own money? Could it be that you resent my generosity?"

Raising Lazarus From the Dead
(John 11:1–45)

Lazarus [not the beggar in the parable] and his sisters, Mary and Martha, lived in Bethany, a small village near Jerusalem. Jesus loved them very much. Then one day Lazarus became ill, so his sisters sent a message to Jesus, who was on the other side of the Jordan River. Even after Jesus heard the news, he stayed there for two more days. He told his disciples, "Our friend Lazarus is asleep, but I'm going to wake him up." The disciples said, "Lord, if he's only resting, he'll be fine." They thought Jesus was just referring to sleep, so Jesus said more plainly, "Lazarus is dead."

By the time Jesus got to Bethany, Lazarus had been dead for four days. After Martha heard that Jesus was coming, she went out to meet him and said, "Lord, if you had been here, Lazarus would not have died." Jesus said, "Your brother will live again. I am the resurrection and the life, those who believe in me, even though they die, will live." When Mary heard Jesus had arrived, she also went out to him and said, "Lord, if you had been here, Lazarus would not have died." When Jesus saw her and others weeping, he was deeply moved and said, "Where have you buried him?" They said, "Come and see." Then Jesus began to weep and they said, "Look at how much he loved Lazarus."

When they got to the grave, which was a small cave with a stone in front of it, Jesus said, "Move the stone away." Martha said, "Lord, he has been dead for four days." But Jesus said, "Didn't I say that if you believed you would see God's glory?" So they moved the stone and Jesus looked upward, in thanks to his Father, and then shouted with a loud voice, "Lazarus, come out!" Then Lazarus walked out, all wrapped in burial clothes. Many of the Jews who had come to the cave saw this miracle and, therefore, believed in Jesus.

Zacchaeus
(Luke 19:1–10)

On his last journey to Jerusalem before his death, Jesus passed through Jericho, where the wealthy tax collector Zacchaeus lived. As Jesus came into town, a large crowd gathered to see him. Zacchaeus was trying to get a glimpse of Jesus, too, but he couldn't see over the crowd because he wasn't very tall. So he ran ahead of the others and climbed a tree which he knew Jesus would pass by. When Jesus got there, he said, "Zacchaeus, come down out of the tree. I'm going to stay at your house today." Zacchaeus quickly climbed down from the tree and happily welcomed Jesus. But others in the crowd who saw what happened said, "Look, Jesus is going to stay with a sinner!"

But Zacchaeus stood among the crowd and said to Jesus, "Lord, I will give half of my possessions to the poor; and if I have cheated people, I will pay them back four times as much." Jesus said, "Today, salvation has come to you. The Son of Man came to seek and save those who are lost."

Entering Jerusalem
(Matthew 21:1–11; Mark 11:1–10; Luke 19:28–44; John 12:12–19)

On the Sunday before Jesus' death [now known as Palm Sunday], Jesus rode from the Mount of Olives to Jerusalem on a young donkey. He did this to fulfill what the prophet Zechariah had said, "Your king is coming to you, humble, and riding on a donkey." Many of the people in Jerusalem cut branches from the palm trees and placed them on the road while others spread their robes on the road, and they shouted, "Hosanna to the Son of David! Blessed is he who comes in the name of the Lord. Hosanna in the highest."

When Jesus got close to the city, he wept over it and said, "If only you could recognize what things make for peace. The day is coming when your enemies will surround and destroy you because you did not recognize that God had come to visit you." Then he went to the temple in the city, and there he healed the blind and lame who came to him.

In the evening Jesus went to Bethany, but every day he went back to the temple to teach the people, who paid careful attention to what he said. However, the chief priests and elders of these people met at the palace of Caiaphas, the high priest, to discuss how they could deceive Jesus, capture him, and kill him because they thought Jesus was undermining their authority and threatening the peace. Then

Judas, one of the twelve disciples, came to them and said, "What will you give me if I betray Jesus and turn him over to you?" They paid him thirty pieces of silver, so from that time on, Judas looked for a chance to betray his master.

Parable of the Wedding Banquet
(Matthew 22:1–14; Luke 14:16–24)

Jesus said, "The kingdom of heaven is like the king who arranged a marriage banquet for his son. He sent his servants to get those who were invited to the wedding, but they would not come. Instead some went to work; some even beat and killed the servants. This outraged the king, and he sent his armies to destroy the murderers and burn their city. Then he said to his servants, 'The wedding banquet is ready but those who were invited were not worthy to come to it. Therefore, go out into the street and invite as many people as you can find.' Soon the house was filled with guests. When the king came in to greet them he saw a man who was not wearing appropriate wedding clothes. 'How did you get in here without a wedding robe?' he asked. The man was speechless. Because the man had not properly prepared himself for the banquet, the king said to his servants: 'Tie his hands and feet and throw him out into the darkness, where there will be weeping and much pain.'"

[Note: The wedding robe has been interpreted in various ways. In Isaiah 61:10 God is described as having clothed us "with the robe of righteousness." It may be that the wedding robe in the parable is to be understood in this way, and that the man's appearance without it meant he refused what the king (God) wished to give—righteousness and salvation.]

Paying Taxes to Caesar
(Matthew 22:15–22; Mark 12:13–17; Luke 20:20–26)

A group of Pharisees and Herodians [supporters of Herod's family] went to ask Jesus a question designed to trap him. They said, "Teacher, we know that you speak truthfully about God. Tell us whether or not it is lawful to pay taxes to Caesar [the Roman Emperor]." [Note: They knew that if Jesus said it was lawful, he would alienate the Jews, who wished to undermine Roman rule of Israel. If he said that it was not lawful, he could be considered a rebel by Roman authorities.] Jesus, aware of their malicious intent, said, "Why are you testing me? Show me a coin." So they brought him a coin. Then Jesus said, "Whose inscription is on it?" They said, "Caesar's." Jesus said, "Give to Caesar that which is Caesar's and to God that which is God's." When they heard what he said, they were amazed at him.

Parable of the Talents
(Matthew 25:14–30; Luke 19:11–27)

Jesus said, "A man going on a long trip called his servants and gave them his money for safekeeping while he was gone. He distributed it according to their ability to manage it. One received just one talent [a large sum of money], one received two talents, and one received five talents. After a long time, the man returned and called the three servants to settle accounts with him. The one who had received five talents came and said, 'Master, you gave me five talents and I have earned five more with them.' His master said to him, 'Well done; you are a good and faithful servant. You did so well managing the little I gave you to do that I will give you much more to manage.' The servant who had received two talents had gained two more; thus the man did likewise with him. Then the one who had received just one talent came and said, 'Master, I know you are a harsh man, so being afraid, I hid your talent in the ground. Here it is.' His master said, 'You wicked and lazy servant! If you knew that I am a hard man to deal with, you should have put my money in the bank so I could at least have received my money back with interest.' And he commanded that the servant's one talent be given to the one with ten talents; because to those who have much, more will be given. The lazy servant was thrown out into the darkness, where there was weeping and much pain."

The Passion Narrative: Jesus' Suffering and Death

Washing the Disciples' Feet
(John 13:1–38)

On the evening before Jesus' crucifixion, Jesus knew that the time for his suffering and death was near. Out of love for his disciples, Jesus poured water into a bowl and began to wash the disciples' feet, wiping them with the towel that was tied around his waist. When he got to Peter, the apostle said, "Lord, are you going to wash my feet?!" Jesus answered, "Right now, you don't know why I'm doing this, but later you'll understand." After he washed all the disciples' feet, Jesus put on his robe, returned to the table, and said to them, "Do you know why I did this? If I, the one you call Lord and Teacher, have washed your feet, you should also wash one another's feet. I did this to set an example for you; I'm giving you a new commandment: love one another just as I have loved you."

[Note: The Gospel of John substitutes this foot washing story for the story of the Last Supper. See below.]

Promising to Send the Holy Spirit
(John 14:25–26)

As part of Jesus' farewell teaching to his disciples, he said, "I have been telling you all these things while I'm still here with you. After I am gone, the Father will send a counselor, the Holy Spirit, to teach you and remind you of all that I told you."

The Last Supper
(Matthew 26:17–29; Mark 14:12–25;
Luke 22:7–38; 1 Corinthians 11:23–26)

The night he was betrayed [the night before he was crucified], Jesus sat down with his twelve disciples to eat the Passover meal. As they were eating, he said, "Truly, I tell you that one of you will betray me." The disciples became upset and each of them said, "Not me!" Jesus answered, "It is the one who is dipping bread into the bowl with me." [Jesus was referring to Judas.]

While they ate, Jesus took a loaf of bread, blessed it, broke it, and gave it to his disciples saying, "Take and eat. This is my body."

Then he took a cup of wine and, after giving thanks, gave it to the disciples and all of them drank from it. Jesus said, "This is my blood of the covenant, which is poured out for many."

Predicting Peter's Denial
(Matthew 26:30–35, Mark 14:26–31; Luke 22:31–34; John 13:36–38)

After the Last Supper, Jesus and the disciples sang a hymn and went out to the Mount of Olives. Jesus said to them, "You will all desert me tonight, but after I am raised [from the dead], I'll meet you in Galilee." Peter said, "Even though all the rest will desert you, I will not." Jesus answered, "Before the rooster crows twice, you will deny me three times." But Peter strongly protested saying, "Even if I have to die with you, I will not deny you." The rest of the disciples said the same thing.

The Garden of Gethsemane
(Matthew 26:36–56; Mark 14:32–52, Luke 22:39–53; John 18:1–12)

When Jesus and the disciples reached the Mount of Olives, they went to a garden called Gethsemane. Jesus said, "Sit here while I go over there and pray." Then he took Peter, James, and John with him farther into the garden. He said to them, "I am deeply saddened. Stay awake with me." Jesus went by himself a bit farther into the garden, fell to the ground, and prayed, "My Father, if it is possible, let this cup [suffering and death] pass from me. Nevertheless, not my will, but your will be done."

Then he returned to the three disciples and found them sleeping. He said to Peter, "What? You couldn't stay awake with me for one hour? Stay awake and pray that you do not face temptation." With that, Jesus went away again and prayed the same words. He prayed two more times, but found the disciples sleeping each time he returned to them. Finally, he woke them up and said, "The time has come when the Son of Man will be betrayed and given into the hands of sinners. Get up; we must go. My betrayer is here."

While he was still speaking, Judas arrived with a large crowd sent from the chief priests, scribes, and elders. They carried swords and clubs. Judas, the betrayer, had told the crowd earlier, "The one I will kiss is the man you want; arrest him and have the guards lead him away." So Judas came to Jesus and said, "Master," and he kissed his cheek. Then the guards arrested him. Jesus said, "Have you come with weapons to arrest me as though I were a robber? I was with you many days in the temple teaching and you didn't arrest me. But the scriptures must be fulfilled." And all the disciples deserted him and fled.

Jesus Before the Council
(Matthew 2 6:57–68; Mark 14:53–65; Luke 22:54a, 63–71; John 18:13–24)

Jesus was brought to the high priest [whose name was Caiaphas], where the chief priests, elders and scribes were assembled. They looked for witnesses to lie about Jesus in order to put him to death, but the witnesses offered conflicting testimony. Then the high priest asked Jesus, "Are you the Messiah?" Jesus answered, "I am; and [as the prophets of long ago said] 'you will see the Son of Man seated at the right hand of Power [God],' and 'coming with the clouds of heaven." Then the high priest tore his own clothes in anger, saying, "Why do we need any witnesses? You have heard his own blasphemy. What have you decided to do with him?" They all answered, "He deserves to die." And some of them spit in his face and mocked him. Then the guards grabbed him and beat him.

Peter's Denial
(Matthew 26:69–75; Mark 14:66–72; Luke 22:54b–62; John 18:15–18, 25–27)

After Jesus was arrested, Peter followed him from a distance until he reached the courtyard of the high priest's palace. A maid there asked him, "You were with Jesus, weren't you?" Peter denied it saying, "I don't know what you're talking about." Then he moved away from her toward the exit from the courtyard. And the rooster crowed once. The same maid saw him again and, pointing at Peter, said to a group of bystanders, "That man was with him." But Peter denied it again. A short time later the bystanders said, "Certainly you are one of his followers. You're a Galilean." Then Peter began to swear and he said, "I don't know this man." At that very moment, the rooster crowed for a second time. Peter remembered that Jesus said to him, "Before the rooster crows twice, you will deny me three times." And Peter broke down and wept.

Judas' Death
(Matthew 27:3–10; Acts 1:16–20)

When Judas, who had betrayed Jesus, saw that Jesus was condemned to death, Judas repented and brought back the thirty pieces of silver to the chief priests. He said to them, "I have sinned by betraying an innocent man." And they said, "What's that to us? That's your problem." So Judas threw the money down and went and hanged himself.

Jesus Before Pontius Pilate
(Matthew 27:1–26; Mark 15:1–15; Luke 23:1–5, 13–25;
John 18:28–19:16)

Early Friday morning, Jesus was brought to the Roman governor, Pontius Pilate. Pilate asked him, "Are you the King of the Jews?" Jesus answered, "You said that I am." Then the chief priests began to accuse Jesus of many things. Pilate asked him, "What is your answer to these charges? Don't you have one?" Jesus said nothing and Pilate was amazed at his silence.

Now it was Pilate's custom during the Passover festival to release one prisoner at the people's request. The crowd came that day expecting Pilate to do so. Pilate asked them, "Do you want me to release the King of the Jews?" (Pilate had realized that Jesus was arrested because the religious leaders were jealous of him, not because of his own wrongdoings.) But the chief priests led the crowd to ask that a man named Barabbas, a murderer, be released instead. Then Pilate asked, "What should I do with the man you have called the King of the Jews?" They shouted, "Crucify him!" Pilate asked, "Why? What has he done?" The crowd didn't answer, other than to shout, "Crucify him!" So to satisfy the crowd Pilate released Barrabas, and, after having Jesus whipped, turned him over to the soldiers for crucifixion.

Jesus' Crucifixion and Death
(Matthew 27:27–56; Mark 15:16–41; Luke 23:26–49; John 19:17–37)

Then the soldiers led Jesus into the courtyard of the governor's palace, where they clothed him in a purple robe and twisted some thorns into the shape of a crown to put on his head. They mocked him with a salute, "Hail, King of the Jews." They beat him, spit on him, and knelt down, derisively pretending to honor him. Then they took off the purple robe, put his own clothes back on him, and led him away to be crucified. They forced someone who was passing by, Simon of Cyrene, to help Jesus carry his cross to Golgotha [also called Calvary], where he was crucified. After nailing Jesus to the cross, the soldiers gambled to see who would win his clothes.

It was nine o'clock in the morning when he was put on the cross, and there were two robbers crucified with him, one on his right side and the other on his left. Over the cross, the soldiers wrote these words: "Jesus of Nazareth, King of the Jews."

[All together, the gospels record seven times that Jesus spoke while he hung on the cross, before he died.] (1) "Father forgive them, they do not know what they are doing." The disciple John stood nearby with Jesus' mother, Mary; his mother's sister; and Mary Magdalene. And Jesus said to his mother, (2) "Woman, here is your son [referring to John]." And to the disciple, "Here is your mother." And from that time, the disciple took her to his home to live with him.

The soldiers and the priests continued to mock Jesus as he hung on the cross. As they were doing so, one of the robbers said, "If you are the Christ, save yourself and us." But the other robber said, "We have been rightly condemned for our deeds, but this man did nothing wrong." And he said to Jesus, "Lord, remember me when you enter your kingdom." Jesus answered, (3) "Truly, today you will be with me in paradise."

At noon darkness spread over the whole land, and it lasted until about three o'clock, when Jesus cried out with a loud voice, (4) "My God, my God, why have you forsaken me?" And then he said, (5) "I thirst." The soldiers offered him some wine; but he didn't take it. Jesus said, (6) "It is finished." Finally, he cried out with a loud voice, saying, (7) "Father, into your hands I commend my spirit." With that, he bowed his head and took his last breath. When the Roman centurion saw how he cried out and what had taken place, he said, "This man was truly the Son of God!"

Jesus' Burial
(Matthew 27:57–61; Mark 15:42–47; Luke 23:50–56; John 19:38–42)

Joseph of Arimathea, a respected member of the religious council, eagerly waited for the kingdom of God to come. It took courage for him to ask Pilate for Jesus' body so that Joseph himself could give Jesus a proper burial. After receiving permission, Joseph brought a linen cloth and took Jesus' body down from the cross. He wrapped the body in the linen cloth and laid it in a tomb carved out of rock. Then he rolled a huge stone in front of it. Mary Magdalene and another woman named Mary saw where Jesus' body was buried.

Resurrection and Ascension

Jesus is Raised From the Dead
(Matthew 28:1–10; Mark 16:1–8; Luke 24:1–12; John 20:1–10)

Three women—Mary Magdalene, Mary the mother of James, and Salome—bought spices so that they could anoint Jesus' body with them. At dawn on Sunday morning [now known as Easter Sunday], they went to the tomb. They asked each other, "Who will roll the huge stone away from the entrance of the tomb for us?" But they discovered that the stone had already been rolled away. Upon entering the tomb, the women were stunned to see a young man wearing a white robe sitting there. He said to them, "Don't be shocked. You're looking for Jesus of Nazareth, who was crucified. He has risen and is not here. Look, this is the place where his body had been laid. Go and tell Peter and the other disciples that Jesus is going ahead of you to Galilee and you will see him there, just as he told you." At this, the women ran out of the tomb because they were terrified and amazed.

Jesus' Appearance to Mary Magdalene [and the other Women] (Matthew 28:9–10; Mark 16:9–11; John 20:14–18)

After he was raised from the dead, Jesus appeared first to Mary Magdalene, the woman from whom he had cast out seven demons.

While she stood near the tomb, Jesus appeared to her, saying, "Why are you weeping?" She did not recognize him and thought he was the gardener. She said to him, "If you have taken him [Jesus] away, tell me where you laid him." Jesus said to her, "Mary." When she heard him say her name she knew it was Jesus and said, "Teacher!" He said, "Go to my disciples and tell them that I am ascending to my Father and your Father, my God and your God." And so she went and told the disciples that she had seen the Lord.

Jesus' Appearance on the Road to Emmaus (Mark 16:12–13; Luke 24:13–35)

On that same Sunday, two of the disciples were on their way from Jerusalem to the village of Emmaus, about seven miles away. As they walked along, talking about all the things that had happened, Jesus himself began to walk with them down the road, but they didn't recognize him. Finally Jesus asked them, "What are you talking about?" They stopped walking, and with sad looks on their faces, they answered, "You must be the only stranger in Jerusalem who doesn't know what happened these past few days. The chief priests and other leaders have crucified Jesus of Nazareth, who was power-ful both for what he said and what he did. We were hoping that he was the one the prophets had promised would come and redeem Israel, but he was crucified three days ago."

"Moreover," they continued, "some women who were at the tomb this morning found his grave empty. They said they saw angels there who told them that he was alive. So some of the disciples went to the tomb, and they found it empty, just as the women said, but they didn't see him."

Then Jesus said to them, "You don't believe what the prophets said! Didn't they say that it was necessary for the Christ to suffer these things before entering into his glory?" Then, beginning with Moses, he went on to explain to them all that had ever been written about himself in the scriptures.

When they neared Emmaus, he walked ahead, as if he planned to keep going. But they urged him not to, saying, "It's getting late; the day is almost over." So he went to stay with them. As he sat at the table with them that evening, he took bread, blessed it, broke it, and gave it to them. Suddenly they realized who he was, but he vanished from their sight. And they said to one another, "As we walked today, it was as if a fire burned within us while he explained the scriptures to us." That same hour they left to return to Jerusalem, where they found the apostles [Jesus' disciples] gathered with some friends. Then they told the group what had happened and how they had recognized Jesus when he broke the bread.

Jesus' Appearance to the Disciples [or the Story of Doubting Thomas] (Luke 24:36–43; John 20:19–29)

Although the disciples were in a locked house because they were afraid of the authorities, while they talked Jesus appeared among them. He said to them, "Peace be with you." Then he showed them his hands with the nail marks and his side that a soldier had pierced with a sword after he died, and they rejoiced at the sight of the risen Lord.

Now one of the disciples, Thomas, was not with them at the time; so when the others told him that they had seen the Lord, he was doubtful. He said, "Unless I put my fmger into the mark of the nails that were in his hands and put my hand in his pierced side, I will not believe."

A week later the disciples were again together in the house with the doors shut, but Jesus appeared and said, "Peace be with you."

However, to Thomas he said, "Look at my hands and touch them. Put your hand in my side. Do not doubt, but believe." Thomas said to him, "My Lord and my God!" Jesus answered, "Do you believe now that you have seen me? Blessed are those who have not seen and yet believe."

Jesus Commissions the Disciples [or The Great Commission] (Matthew 28:16–20; Mark 16:15–16, 20; Luke 24:44–49)

Jesus appeared to the eleven remaining disciples [Judas was dead] and said, "All authority in heaven and on earth has been given to me. Therefore, go to every nation and make disciples of the people, baptizing them in the name of the Father, and of the Son, and of the Holy Spirit. And teach them to obey all that I have commanded."

Jesus' Ascension to Heaven (Mark 16:19; Luke 24:50–51; Acts 1:6–11)

For forty days Jesus appeared to the disciples and spoke to them about things pertaining to the kingdom of God. Then he took them to the Mount of Olives. There he lifted up his hands, blessed the disciples, and was taken up into heaven on a cloud, as the disciples looked on. While they looked intently upward, two men in white robes came and stood by them and said, "This same Jesus who was taken up into heaven will come back again in the same way you just saw him go into heaven."

The Apostles

[Note: Jesus' twelve disciples were often called apostles, especially after Jesus sent them out to preach the gospel throughout the world. The word apostle comes from a Greek verb which means 'to send out.' Although Paul was not among Jesus' original disciples, he was considered an apostle because the risen Jesus Christ appeared to him and sent him to preach the Gospel to the Gentiles.]

Sending the Holy Spirit [Pentecost]
(Acts 1:1–5, 12–26; Acts 2:1–47)

At his ascension, Jesus had told the disciples, "You will receive the power of the Holy Spirit when it comes upon you and you'll become my witnesses in Jerusalem, Judea and Samaria, and throughout the world." Until they received the Holy Spirit, they were told not to leave Jerusalem.

After Jesus' ascension, they returned to Jerusalem from the Mount of Olives. The eleven remaining apostles had prayed that the Lord would show them who was to be chosen to take the place of Judas. A man named Matthias was chosen. Now all twelve apostles were together on the morning of Pentecost [a Jewish festival held fifty days after the Passover], ten days after Jesus ascended to heaven. Suddenly a sound like a mighty wind came from heaven and it filled the whole house where they were gathered. Then, a tongue of fire appeared and divided itself, with one tongue resting on each of the apostles. At that moment, they were all filled with the Holy Spirit and began to speak.

Now at that time, Jews from every country lived in Jerusalem. When they were able to hear what the apostles said in their own languages, they were bewildered. They asked, "What is happening? Aren't these men [the apostles] from the same country, Galilee? How is it that they can speak about the great works of God to all of us in our native languages?" Then Peter stood up and said, "Jesus of Nazareth, whom you crucified, is now sitting at the right hand of God, and has sent the Holy Spirit to us." They said, "What should we do?" And Peter answered, "Repent and be baptized in the name of Jesus Christ for the forgiveness of sins and you will receive the gift of the Holy Spirit."

So on that day there were about 3,000 who were baptized. The faithful came together daily to pray and to receive the Lord's Supper. They sold their goods, and divided the proceeds among the people, according to their needs. And every day the Lord added believers to the church.

[Note: Since this time, Christians have celebrated Pentecost as the day God sent the Holy Spirit to the apostles.]

Peter and John Before the Council
(Acts 3–5)

One day the apostles Peter and John went to the temple to pray. A man who was lame from birth sat outside the temple gate and asked those entering for gifts of money. Peter said to him, "I don't have any silver or gold, but what I do have I'll give to you. In Jesus' name, stand up and walk." And immediately the man jumped up, walked with them into the temple, and praised God. And many more who saw this believed and were baptized.

Finally, the priests and scribes arrested the apostles for healing the lame man and teaching people that the dead will be resurrected in Jesus' name. They brought the apostles before the ruling Council members who said, "We gave you strict orders not to teach about Jesus, yet you're doing it anyway!" Peter answered, "We must obey God rather than people."

When the Council members heard this they were very angry and wanted to kill the apostles, but Gamaliel, a Pharisee who was respected by all of them, said, "Leave these men alone. If their teaching is of human origin, it will amount to nothing. But if it is of God, you will not be able to overthrow them. In that case, you would be trying to fight God!" He convinced them not to kill the apostles, but instead they whipped them and again ordered them not to teach in the name of Jesus. As the apostles left the Council, they rejoiced that they were considered worthy of suffering shame for the name of Jesus; and they continued to teach and preach that Jesus is the Messiah.

Stephen
(Acts 6:1–8:1)

Because the number of believers was growing so rapidly, the apostles appointed seven men who were wise and full of the Holy Spirit to help them. One of these was Stephen, who worked miracles among the people. Some scribes argued with Stephen, but they were no match for the wisdom and spirit with which he spoke. So they brought him before the Council and arranged for witnesses to lie about him. The false witnesses said, "We heard him speak blasphemy against both Moses and God." In response, Stephen explained how, through the generations, the people of Israel had often turned away from God and resisted the Holy Spirit. When the scribes heard what he said, they were enraged; but Stephen, filled with the Holy Spirit, looked up to heaven and said, "I see the heavens opening, and the Son of Man is standing at God's right hand." With that they rushed to seize him. Then they dragged him out of the city and threw stones at him. While they did this, Stephen prayed, "Lord Jesus, receive my spirit!" And kneeling down, he cried loudly, "Lord, do not hold this sin against them!" Having said this, he died. And Saul, a young man who had agreed to watch over the coats of those who stoned Stephen, approved of what they did.

[Note: Stephen was the first Christian who died because of his faith in Christ. Such people are called martyrs.]

Cornelius
(Acts 10:1–11:18)

Although Jesus had told his apostles to teach people of every nation about what they learned from him, at first they preached only to Jews because they did not yet understand that the Gentiles were also to be taught about the kingdom of God.

One day, while the apostle Peter was praying, he had a vision. He saw something that looked like a large sheet coming down from heaven. There were all kinds of animals, reptiles, and birds on it. Then he heard a voice say, "Get up, Peter. Kill what you want and eat it." But Peter answered, "No, Lord. I have never eaten anything that is considered unclean according to Jewish law." The voice said, "Do not call unclean what God has cleansed." This happened three times, and then the sheet was taken back up into heaven.

While Peter pondered what his vision meant, men arrived who had been sent by a Gentile named Cornelius, a Roman centurion. Peter went with the men, as they asked, and preached to Cornelius as well as his relatives and servants. While Peter spoke to them, the Holy Spirit filled all who heard the words. And Peter, understanding his vision, asked, "Can we withhold the water of baptism from anyone who has received the Holy Spirit, just as we have?" So they were baptized in the name of the Lord. When the believers in Jerusalem heard what had happened, they said, "Then God has granted repentance to the Gentiles as well as the Jews."

Paul
(Acts 9:1–31; Acts 12–28)

Saul, who had witnessed the stoning of Stephen, continued to threaten the Christians. He went to the high priest and obtained legal papers that said if he found any Jews in Damascus who were Christians, he could arrest them and return them to Jerusalem. As he neared Damascus, a flash of light from heaven suddenly surrounded him, and he fell to the ground. He heard a voice saying, "Saul, Saul, why are you persecuting me?" He answered, "Who are you?" And the Lord said, "I am Jesus, the one you are persecuting. Get up and go into the city. Once you are there, you will be told what to do." Saul got up, but he was blind, so the men traveling with him had to lead him by the hand.

Now there was a disciple named Ananias in Damascus. The Lord told him in a vision, "Go to Saul and lay your hands on him so his sight is restored." Ananias answered, "I have heard about this man Saul and how cruel he has been to believers in Jerusalem." But the Lord said, "Go to him because he is the one I have chosen to preach my name to the Gentiles." So Ananias went and put his hands on Saul. Immediately something like scales fell from Saul's eyes and his sight was restored. Then Saul went to be baptized, and he preached about Christ in the synagogues, saying that Jesus was the Son of God. Saul's name was changed to Paul, and he was called by God to be an apostle.

[Note: Paul made three great missionary journeys, and he has been called 'the apostle to the Gentiles.' During one of his journeys, he preached in Antioch in the region of Syria. This is where believers in Jesus were first called Christians. He also went to Greece, spreading the Gospel. Paul wrote a number of letters to churches and individuals which appear in the New Testament. Keys verses from these letters, as well as others from the New Testament, are quoted from the NRSV Bible in the next section.]

The Letters

Key Verses From Paul's Letters

"Love is patient; love is kind; love is not envious or boastful or arrogant or rude. It does not insist on its own way; it is not irritable or resentful; it does not rejoice in wrongdoing, but rejoices in the truth. It bears all things, believes all things, hopes all things, endures all things." *(1 Corinthians 13:4–7)*

"Such is the confidence that we have through Christ toward God. Not that we are competent of ourselves to claim anything as coming from us; our competence is from God, who has made us competent to be ministers of a new covenant, not of letter but of spirit; for the letter kills, but the Spirit gives life." *(2 Corinthians 3;4–6)*

". . . we know that a person is justified not by the works of the law but through faith in Jesus Christ. And we have come to believe in Christ Jesus, so that we might be justified by faith in Christ, and not by doing the works of the law, because no one will be justified by the works of the law. For through the law I died to the law, so that I might live to God. I have been crucified with Christ; and it is no longer I who live, but it is Christ who lives in me. And the life I now live in the flesh I live by faith in the Son of God, who loved me and gave himself for me." *(Galatians 2:16–20)*

"If then there is any encouragement in Christ, any consolation from love, any sharing in the Spirit, any compassion and sympathy, make my joy complete: be of the same mind, having the same love, being in full accord and of one mind. Do nothing from selfish ambition or conceit, but in humility regard others as better than yourselves. Let each of you look not to your own interests, but to the interests of others. Let the same mind be in you that was in Christ Jesus, who, though he was in the form of God, did not regard equality with God as something to be exploited, but emptied himself, taking the form of a slave, being born in human likeness. And being found in human form, he humbled himself and became obedient to the point of death—even death on a cross. Therefore God also highly exalted him and gave him the name that is above every name, so that at the name of Jesus every knee should bend, in heaven and on earth and under the earth, and every tongue should confess that Jesus Christ is Lord, to the glory of God the Father." *(Philippians 2:1–11)*

"For I am not ashamed of the gospel; it is the power of God for salvation to everyone who has faith, to the Jew first and also to the Greek. For in it the righteousness of God is revealed through faith for faith; as it is written, 'The one who is righteous will live by faith.'" *(Romans 1:16–17)*

"But now, apart from law, the righteousness of God has been disclosed, and is attested by the law and the prophets, the righteousness of God through faith in Jesus Christ for all who believe. For there is no distinction, since all have sinned and fall short of the glory of God; they are now justified by his grace as a gift, through the redemption that is in Christ Jesus, whom God put forward as a sacrifice of atonement by his blood, effective through faith. He did this to show his righteousness, because in his divine forbearance he had passed over the sins previously committed; it was to prove at the present time that he himself is righteous and that he justifies the one who has faith in Jesus." *(Romans 3:21–26)*

"Do you not know that all of us who have been baptized into Christ Jesus were baptized into his death? Therefore we have been buried with him by baptism into death, so that, just as Christ was raised from the dead by the glory of the Father, so we too might walk in newness of life. For if we have been united with him in a death like his, we will certainly be united with him in a resurrection like his. We know that our old self was crucified with him so that the body of sin might be destroyed, and we might no longer be enslaved to sin." *(Romans 6:3–6)*

"Who will separate us from the love of Christ? Will hardship, or distress, or persecution, or famine, or nakedness, or peril, or sword? . . . No, in all these things we are more than conquerors through him who loved us. For I am convinced that neither death, nor life, nor angels, nor rulers, nor things present, nor things to come, nor powers, nor height, nor depth, nor anything else in all creation, will be able to separate us from the love of God in Christ Jesus our Lord." *(Romans 8:35, 37–39)*

"So faith comes from what is heard, and what is heard comes through the word of Christ." *(Romans 10:17)*

Key Verses From Other Letters

"Now faith is the assurance of things hoped for, the conviction of things not seen." *(Hebrews 11:1)*

"You have been born anew, not of perishable but of imperishable seed, through the living and enduring word of God. For 'All flesh is like grass and all its glory like the flower of grass. The grass withers, and the flower falls, but the word of the Lord endures forever.' That word is the good news that was announced to you." *(1 Peter 1:23–25)*

"If we say that we have no sin, we deceive ourselves, and the truth is not in us. If we confess our sins, he who is faithful and just will forgive us our sins and cleanse us from all unrighteousness." *(1 John 1:8–9)*

"God's love was revealed among us in this way: God sent his only Son into the world so that we might live through him. In this is love, not that we loved God but that he loved us and sent his Son to be the atoning sacrifice for our sins. Beloved, since God loved us so much, we also ought to love one another." *(1 John 4:9–11)*

The Revelation to John

[Note: In the broadest sense of the word, the entire Bible can be referred to as God's revelation, but the Book of Revelation is a type of literature called apocalyptic. Apocalyptic literature is found in the Old Testament (e.g., the Book of Daniel; and Ezekiel, chapters 38–39), in sections of the New Testament (e.g., Mark, chapter 13), and in non-Biblical Christian and Jewish writings which first appeared in the third century before Christ. The content of such literature tells, in vivid imagery, about the end times. Some interpret the Book of Revelation very literally, while others view it as purely symbolic as to what the end of the world will be like. Because of the vast differences in interpretation, the verses included below are quoted from the Book of Revelation, NRSV Bible.]

Armageddon

"And they [demonic spirits] assembled them [the kings of the whole world] at the place that in Hebrew is called Harmagedon [Armageddon]." *(Revelation 16:16)*

[Note: The above verse is the only verse in the Book of Revelation which mentions Armageddon, but it has become a powerful word, which people still use today to refer to the cosmic end of human history and all creation.]

A New Heaven and a New Earth

"Then I [John] saw a new heaven and a new earth; for the first heaven and the first earth had passed away, and the sea was no more. And I saw the holy city, the new Jerusalem, coming down out of heaven from God, prepared as a bride adorned for her husband. And I heard a loud voice from the throne saying, 'See, the home of God is among mortals. He will dwell with them as their God; they will be his peoples, and God himself will be with them; he will wipe every tear from their eyes. Death will be no more; mourning and crying and pain will be no more, for the first things have passed away.' And the one who was seated on the throne said, 'See, I am making all things new.' Also he said, 'Write this, for these words are trustworthy and true.' Then he said to me, 'It is done! I am the Alpha and the Omega, the beginning and the end. To the thirsty I will give water as a gift from the spring of the water of life." *(Revelation 21:1–15)*

Conclusion of the Book of Revelation and the Bible

"The one who testifies to these things says, 'Surely I am coming soon., Amen. Come, Lord Jesus! The grace of the Lord Jesus be with all the saints. Amen." *(Revelation 22:20–21)*

Books of the New Testament

Matthew
Mark
Luke
John
Acts of the Apostles
Romans
I & II Corinthians
Galatians
Ephesians
Philippians
Colossians

I & II Thessalonians
I & II Timothy
Titus
Philemon
Hebrews
James
I & II Peter
I, II & III John
Jude
Revelation

New Testament Timeline

[Note: All dates provided below are speculative; however, the specific dates in parentheses are based on more convincing historical evidence.]

50   Herod the Great, ruler of Galilee and Palestine (40 B.C. to 4 B.C.)

Augustus Caesar, Emperor of Rome (43 B.C. to 14 A.D.)

Jesus is born (between 6 B.C. and 4 B.C.)

A.D.

Activity of John the Baptist (28 to 29 A.D.)

Pontius Pilate, Roman Governor of Palestine (26 A.D. to 36 A.D.)

Jesus is Crucified (30 A.D.)

Conversion of Paul (32A.D.)

Persecution of Christians in Jerusalem (43 to 44 A.D.)

Council of the Apostles in Jerusalem (50 A.D.)

50   Paul arrives in Corinth, Greece (50 A.D.)

Paul stays in Ephesus (53 A.D.)

Paul is back in Jerusalem and is arrested (56 A.D.)

Paul taken prisoner in Jerusalem and moved to Caesarea and, finally, to Rome (58 to 60 A.D.)

Emperor Nero persecutes Christians in Rome (64 A.D.)

[Note: Peter and Paul might have been martyred in Rome during this persecution.]

Destruction of Jerusalem by the Romans (70 A.D.)

Persecution of Christians in Rome under Emperor Domitian (95 A.D.)

Appendix

The Lord's Prayer

The Lord's Prayer is given in two forms. On the left is the most familiar form, which is from the language of the King James Version of the Bible. On the right is a contemporary version of the Lord's Prayer. [Note: The words in italics, collectively known as the doxology, are an addition to the Lord's Prayer which is not found in the Bible.]

Our Father who art in heaven
    hallowed by thy name, thy
    kingdom come, thy will be done,
    on earth as it is in heaven.
Give us this day our daily bread;
    and forgive us our trespasses, as
    we forgive those who
    trespass against us.
And lead us not into temptation,
    but deliver us from evil.
For thine is the kingdom, and the
    power, and the glory, forever and
    ever. Amen.

Our Father in heaven, hal-
    lowed be your name, your
    kingdom come, your will be
    done, on earth as in heaven.
Give us today our daily bread.
    Forgive us our sins
    as we forgive those who sin
    against us.
Save us from the time of trial
    and deliver us from evil.
For the kingdom, the power, and
    the glory are yours, now and
    forever. Amen.

The Apostles' Creed and the Nicene Creed

The Apostles' Creed and the Nicene Creed are not found in the Bible, but are helpful as brief statements of the Christian faith. Notice how the Christian understanding of God as "Trinity" (one God in three persons) is stated, especially in the Nicene Creed.

The Apostles' Creed (150 A.D.)

I believe in God, the Father almighty,
    creator of heaven and earth.
I believe in Jesus Christ, his only Son, our Lord.
    He was conceived by the power of the Holy Spirit
        and born of the virgin Mary.
    He suffered under Pontius Pilate,
        was crucified, died, and was buried. He descended into hell.
    On the third day he rose again.
    He ascended into heaven,
        and is seated at the right hand of the Father.
    He will come again to judge the living and the dead.
I believe in the Holy Spirit,
    the holy catholic Church,
    the communion of saints,
    the forgiveness of sins,
    the resurrection of the body,
    and the life everlasting. Amen.

The Nicene Creed (325 A.D.)

We believe in one God,
 the Father, the Almighty,
 maker of heaven and earth,
 of all that is seen and unseen.
We believe in one Lord, Jesus Christ,
 the only Son of God,
 eternally begotten of the Father
 God from God, Light from Light,
 true God from true God,
 begotten, not made,
 of one Being with the Father.
 Through him all things were made.
 For us and for our salvation
  he came down from heaven;
   by the power of the Holy Spirit
    he became incarnate from the virgin Mary,
     and was made man.
For our sake he was crucified under Pontius Pilate;
 he suffered death and was buried.
On the third day he rose again
 in accordance with the Scriptures;
he ascended into heaven
 and is seated at the right hand of the Father.
He will come again in glory to judge the living and the
  dead,
 and his kingdom will have no end.
We believe in the Holy Spirit, the Lord, the giver of life,
 who proceeds from the Father and the Son.
 With the Father and the Son he is worshiped and glorified.
 He has spoken through the prophets.
 We believe in one holy catholic and apostolic Church.
 We acknowledge one Baptism for the forgiveness of sins.
 We look for the resurrection of the dead,
  and the life of the world to come. Amen.

Index